By Simon Lelic:

The Haven
The Haven: Revolution

And for adult readers:

The Liar's Room
The House
The Child Who
The Facility
Rupture

THE
HAVEN

SIMON LELIC

HODDER

HODDER CHILDREN'S BOOKS

First published in Great Britain in 2019 by Hodder and Stoughton

1 3 5 7 9 10 8 6 4 2

Text copyright © Simon Lelic, 2019

The moral rights of the author have been asserted.

A CIP catalogue record for this book
is available from the British Library.

ISBN 978 1 444 94760 1

Typeset in Adobe Garamond by Hewer Text UK Ltd, Edinburgh
Printed and bound in Great Britain by Clays Ltd, Elcograf S.p.A

The paper and board used in this book
are made from wood from responsible sources.

Hodder Children's Books
An imprint of
Hachette Children's Group
Part of Hodder and Stoughton
Carmelite House
50 Victoria Embankment
London EC4Y 0DZ

An Hachette UK Company
www.hachette.co.uk

www.hachettechildrens.co.uk

FOR BANJO

╫ PROLOGUE

Maddy Sikes picked up the telephone, confident it was the call she'd been expecting. 'Is it done?'

'It's done,' replied the voice.

'The woman?'

'The woman. The kid, too.'

'The kid?'

'She wasn't alone. There was a kid there as well. But relax. It's been taken care of.'

Sikes pressed her fingertips to the bridge of her nose. 'You killed a kid. I never told you to kill a kid.'

'I didn't say I killed the kid. What I said was, the kid's been taken care of.'

'Wait,' said Sikes. 'You *didn't* kill the kid? You left him, her, whoever – you left it alive? What the hell am I paying you for?'

'Him. I left him alive. But relax, would you? I told you it's sorted and it is. You're safe, I promise you. Your precious shipment, too. This thing – the cops, the investigation, even the kid. Believe me when I tell you: it's over.'

1 NIGHT TERRORS

Ollie Turner was asleep when the men came.

They were dressed in black and wearing balaclavas. Before Ollie knew what was happening, they pulled him from his bed and dragged him across the carpet towards the landing.

'Hey!'

Ollie caught a glimpse of a shorter man watching from the stairs. Ollie couldn't see his face, but from the way the man was standing – arms crossed, feet apart – Ollie could tell he was in charge.

Ollie wriggled, but it did no good. He called for Nancy, his guardian, and one of the men clamped a hand around his mouth. In the distance he heard a muffled cry, and Ollie could tell the men had got Nancy, too. She was already being bundled towards the door of their flat. Ollie was an afterthought, it seemed. A loose end. Nancy was the one the men had come for.

They must have been good to catch Nancy unawares. Ollie's guardian was a policewoman, and an expert at everything she did. But somehow these men had taken her captive. What did they want from her?

At the top of the staircase one of the men picked Ollie up, throwing him across his shoulder the way Ollie remembered his father doing when Ollie was young. Ollie tried to yell for help, but it was all he could do through the gag just to breathe. At some point they'd managed to bind his hands behind his back, and the man held his legs to stop him from kicking.

There was a van waiting for them on the street outside, parked at an angle over the kerb. The rear doors were open, like a gaping mouth, and the man got ready to throw Ollie inside. Ollie caught a glimpse of Nancy already sprawled in the back of the vehicle. She was bound like him, around her ankles as well as her hands, and didn't appear to be moving.

'Nancy,' Ollie tried to say, but when the man threw him into the van beside her, Ollie's head hit the metal floor and the world, abruptly, went black.

When Ollie awoke, the ground beneath him was cold and hard, and his hands remained bound behind his back. He wasn't in the van any more, but in a room he didn't recognise. No windows, bare walls and a dusty grey concrete floor.

Nancy was lying just beside him. She was facing away, and she wasn't moving.

'Nancy!' Ollie hissed, desperately.

Nancy had brought Ollie up since he was seven years old, since the day his real parents had been killed in a terrorist attack.

Six years on, Nancy was the person Ollie cared for most in the entire world, and the only person, he would have said, who truly cared for him.

When Nancy didn't respond, Ollie clumsily shuffled upright. He managed to get his feet from under him, and wriggled until he was sitting.

'Nancy!' Ollie said again. He kept his voice low, wary of letting his captors know he'd woken up. They wouldn't be far away, Ollie was certain, and even the slightest noise might bring them back.

He tried nudging his guardian with his knees, and spoke again into her ear.

'Nancy! Wake up. Please, Nancy. You have to wake up!'

Nothing. Nancy didn't even moan.

Ollie was crying, he realised. 'Please, Nancy,' he repeated, not caring now about how loudly he spoke. He didn't even care about the men any more, he just wanted Nancy to show him that she was all right.

'Nancy. Nancy!'

This time, finally, Nancy responded. She let out a whimper, and attempted to roll on to her back. When Ollie said her name again, she came around far more quickly than Ollie had.

'Ollie? Is that . . . is that you? Where are we? Are you OK? Are you hurt?'

'No, I . . .' Even as he spoke Ollie winced at a stabbing pain in his head. He must have hit it hard when he'd been thrown into the van. 'Nancy, you need to sit up,' he said. 'We need to get out of here. Those men, they'll—'

As if on cue, Ollie heard voices from outside the room. There were two doors, he saw, one ahead of him and another behind, with neither offering a clue to where they led.

Nancy had heard the voices, too. She rolled herself upright, with far more agility than Ollie had shown. 'Turn around, Ollie. Put your back to mine.'

Ollie didn't pause to ask questions. He did as Nancy had instructed and immediately he could feel her fingers picking at the knot that was trapping his wrists. She was working blind, but in seconds Ollie found his hands free.

'Now untie me,' Nancy said. 'Work fast, Ollie,' she added, as once again they heard voices outside the door.

Ollie looked at the rope around Nancy's wrists and couldn't believe she had untied him so quickly. The knot in front of him was an inscrutable riddle of cord.

'Hurry, Ollie. They're coming.'

Ollie picked at the rope with his fingernails, but he couldn't work the slightest gap.

'I can't, Nancy! The knot, it's too tight!'

Nancy spun to face him. 'Try the rope around my feet.'

Ollie did, but if anything the knot here was tighter still. He scrabbled with his fingers, felt one of his fingernails break. It was no good. He started looking around for something sharp he might use to cut the rope. The room was empty, the floor bare, but even a piece of glass might do, or a bit of metal, or—

'Ollie? Ollie. Look at me, Ollie.'

Ollie stopped moving. In the silence they heard voices right outside.

'Run. Do you hear me, Ollie? You need to run.'

'But—'

'Run, Ollie! Now. Go!'

Ollie shook his head. He felt tears jostle free as he did so. 'I won't leave you. I won't!'

His vision blurred and he wiped his eyes. Nancy was smiling.

'I love you, Ollie Turner. With all my heart. And if you love me you'll do as I ask. Run, Ollie. *Please.*'

The door ahead of them cracked open. The men were here, now. Ollie had time to let out one final sob, and then he ran.

He wasn't three steps through the door opposite when he heard the shots.

Every instinct told Ollie to stop, to turn around, to go back. *Nancy. Oh, Nancy.* But it was his guardian's voice, in his head, that kept him running. *Go!* she'd said. *Please.*

He wouldn't let her down. He couldn't.

After the shots he heard a shout behind him, and then the rapid pound of boot steps. Ollie reckoned he had a twenty-metre head start at best.

7

As he ran Ollie tried to take in his surroundings, to get a clue about where he should be heading. The corridor he found himself in was one long, anonymous passageway. His best guess was that he was in the office part of a factory of some kind. Something industrial, anyway, where nobody cared much what the building looked like.

He rounded a corner, and heard more men approaching from up ahead. There was a door in the corridor with a key in the lock, and Ollie realised it was his only option.

He unlocked the door and peeked inside. The door opened on to the top of a wooden staircase. There was no light on, and no sight or sound of anyone within, just the steps shearing off into the darkness below.

Ollie swallowed. Even at thirteen years old, he was afraid of the dark – but he was afraid of men with guns, on balance, slightly more. He stepped across the threshold and, before the men could have seen him, closed the door and turned the key.

He exhaled. The air felt thick, unbreathed, and there was a smell like the week-old contents of his gym bag.

All at once the door started shaking. Someone on the other side was trying the handle.

Ollie backed away from the door and his left foot slipped into a void. He looked down and realised he'd reached the edge of the platform at the top of the staircase.

He flailed and felt his fingertips scrape brickwork. His other hand hooked around a wooden stair pole and somehow he managed to haul himself upright. His heart thumping, he looked below him to try to see where he would have fallen – and almost slipped again when, in the darkness, he saw another pair of eyes staring up. Gollum eyes, Ollie found himself thinking, picturing the character from *The Lord of the Rings*. And not the funny Gollum either. The mean one. The one with the teeth.

Ollie yelped. He scrabbled away from the top of the staircase, pressing his back against the door. It clattered in its frame as the eyes below him vanished.

He clamped a hand across his mouth, but too late. Voices filtered through from the corridor outside.

'In here. I thought I heard something.'

'Well, open it up then!'

'I can't find the key. It should be in the lock.'

The key. Ollie unclenched his right hand from around his mouth and realised it was empty. He must have dropped the key when he'd lost his balance. How on earth was he supposed to get out now?

A crash against the door behind him was his answer. Ollie didn't need to worry about breaking out. Whoever was out there was intent on breaking in.

'*Oof.*'

'Harder. Put your shoulder into it.'

This time the door trembled so much Ollie was sure it was about to give way.

The door reverberated with the force of another blow and this time the frame split all the way to the floor. One more thrust, Ollie reckoned, and they would be through.

Ollie crouched, preparing to throw himself at the men . . . but the final thrust never came.

Instead he heard, 'What was that?'

Silence, followed by a noise somewhere in the distance.

Then, 'Over there. Quick!'

The men outside thundered off. Ollie let out the breath he didn't know he'd been holding. He was safe, he realised. For the time being at least. That was what he thought, until the door burst open. Ollie flinched and staggered away. When he turned back he saw a man grinning in the doorway, gleefully staring down at what he'd caught.

2 INTO DARKNESS

Ollie didn't want to fight, but he would if he had to.

The thought of what these men had done to Nancy only fed his anger. But when he set himself to drive forwards, to punch his shoulder into the man's solar plexus, he realised it wasn't a man at all. The owner of the grin was a boy, like him. Older, yes, by maybe two or three years, but a boy nonetheless. He had fair hair, kind eyes and a scar that ran from his left ear almost to his chin.

'Sorry,' the boy said. 'Didn't have time to warn you to stand back. You OK? Good. Then let's go. *Now*.'

The boy spun away. Ollie, open mouthed, was left staring at his retreating back.

When he noticed Ollie wasn't following, the boy turned around.

'I said, let's *go*. They'll be coming back, you know. Those men? It won't take them long to realise the noise they heard was only a distraction.' When Ollie didn't react, the boy extended his hand. 'I'm Dodge, by the way,' he said.

Ollie, automatically, reached out with his own. 'I'm . . . Ollie. I—'

But Ollie didn't have time to finish his sentence. Dodge gripped Ollie's hand and wrenched him through the doorway into the corridor.

'Who are you?' Ollie panted as they ran. 'Where did you come from?'

Dodge glanced at him sideways. 'No time to explain,' he puffed.

They reached a corner and Dodge slowed and spread a hand across Ollie's chest. The older boy peeked around the bend. 'Clear,' he said. 'Let's go.'

They seemed to be heading back the way Ollie had come, but Dodge took them down a turn-off Ollie hadn't realised he'd passed.

'Wait.' Once again Dodge pressed Ollie back. There was a junction ahead, and a man with a gun ran right across their path. He didn't see them. He was too busy listening to the voices crackling on his radio receiver.

'All clear,' said Dodge, and he tried to pull Ollie along.

This time Ollie resisted.

'We have to go back,' he said.

Dodge stumbled to a standstill ahead of him. 'What? What are you talking about?'

'Nancy . . . We have to go back. We have to make sure she's . . . to see if she's . . .'

Dodge checked quickly behind him. When he was sure

there was nobody coming, he drew closer and placed a hand on Ollie's shoulder.

'That woman,' he said. 'She was something to do with you?'

Ollie could feel the tears prickle his eyes. He nodded.

Dodge winced. 'Was she . . . your mum?'

'Not my mum,' Ollie managed to say. 'My friend.'

For half a moment Dodge closed his eyes. He sighed.

'She was a policewoman,' Ollie said. 'I think that's why she . . . why they . . .'

He shook his head to clear it.

'I have to go back,' Ollie insisted. 'I'm not leaving her. I *won't*.'

'Ollie, listen to me.' Dodge stooped slightly so that he and Ollie were roughly the same height. 'There's nothing we can do for her. Not now.'

'But if there's a chance . . .'

'There's no chance, Ollie. Do you hear me? There's no chance. I'm sorry.'

Ollie wriggled himself free of Dodge's grip. He could feel himself shaking his head, trying to deny what the older boy was telling him.

She couldn't be dead. She just *couldn't* be.

'I was in the air-conditioning duct,' Dodge said. 'I saw everything. We've been keeping tabs on what's going on here,' he added, when he noticed Ollie's confusion. 'Look, it's complicated. I'll explain it all to you later. For the moment we need to concentrate on getting out of here. Agreed?'

Ollie hesitated . . . but then he nodded.

They took the next corner, and the next. They passed from the labyrinth of corridors on to what Ollie guessed was the factory floor, and here there were plenty of places for them to hide. There were people shifting crates and manoeuvring forklifts. They were unarmed as far as Ollie could tell, and focused on what they were doing. No one seemed particularly on the lookout – for escaped prisoners or anything else.

Dodge led them at a crouch between the stacks of pallets. As before he seemed to know where he was going. There was a fire door in the far corner and Ollie guessed they were making for that.

'What's in these boxes?' Ollie whispered as they moved.

Dodge frowned, as though he'd been wondering the same thing himself. 'To be honest I'm not sure. They're not her usual type of shipment.'

'Whose usual type of shipment?'

'Maddy Sikes. She owns this place.'

Who's Maddy Sikes? Ollie was about to ask, but it was then that he spotted one of the guards. The workers hadn't been on the lookout because other people were, he realised. And now he'd spotted one, he saw several: people who weren't involved with any of the labour, but instead were standing around the central perimeter, facing out with weapons at the ready. Whatever was in these boxes, it was obviously precious.

They waited until the closest guard turned his back, then dashed to the next point of cover.

'Who *are* these people?' Ollie said. 'You said you were watching them. Why? And what did they want with me? What did they want with Nancy?'

'Your friend was a cop, right?' Dodge answered.

'Right,' Ollie said, trying not to think about the tense Dodge had used. *Was a cop. Not is.*

'What was she? On a task force or something?'

'I . . .' Ollie wasn't sure. All he knew was that Nancy had been a detective of some kind.

Dodge didn't appear to notice that Ollie hadn't answered his question. As they trotted onwards he pulled out a phone. An old iPhone, Ollie thought, but it seemed to have been modified in some way, so that from the Lightning connector there was an antenna attached.

Dodge thumbed a message and tucked the phone back into his pocket.

'Help's on the way,' he said. 'Now we just need to get outside.'

Keeping low they moved towards the fire door, only pausing as they crossed between the rows of pallets to check for guards.

'Right ahead. Almost there, Ollie. We just need to hope that the fire door isn't . . .'

They reached the fire exit and Dodge, without hesitating, shoved down on the metal bar. As soon as the door broke contact with the frame, the air was filled with a piercing electronic scream.

'Alarmed,' Dodge finished, swallowing.

Ollie turned and saw a guard spot them and raise his gun.

'Hey! Stop!'

'Go!'

Dodge shoved Ollie through the doorway before the guard could fire. They bundled outside, and Ollie had barely a moment to register it was daybreak. In his mind it had still been dark outside. Instead, the sun was edging above the horizon, bringing with it a warm, candyfloss glow.

They dashed across the factory yard, dodging another forklift truck as they ran. There was no one behind them, not yet, but as far as Ollie could see they were no better off out here than they had been inside. The factory was on the bank of the Thames, but all around the yard there was a fence at least triple Ollie's height, barricading their access to the river. Topping the fence was a roll of barbed wire.

'What now?' he yelled in panic.

Dodge led Ollie around a corner and pointed to a solid brick wall. 'This way.'

'But . . . we'll be trapped!'

Dodge gave Ollie a look then, though Ollie couldn't tell whether it was a grimace or a grin.

They slid between a parked lorry and the wall, and pressed their backs against the brickwork.

Ollie peeked out from behind the lorry's tyre. 'What now?' he repeated, looking out across the yard. There were men some distance away, searching blindly, but heading steadily in their direction. 'We can't just sit and wait for them to—'

Ollie turned around and realised Dodge had vanished.

'Dodge?' he hissed urgently. '*Dodge*. Where are you?'

He felt panic building from his stomach and for a moment he thought he would be sick. But then a hand closed around his ankle and Ollie, jerking, looked down.

Dodge was peering up at him from a hole in the ground. Beside him, slid to one side, was a manhole cover.

'Are you coming?' Dodge said. 'Or did you want to stay and play with your new friends?'

Ollie tried to peer past Dodge into the darkness below. He couldn't see much, but he could smell plenty.

'What's that stench?' he said, wrinkling his nose. 'Is that a sewer?'

'It is indeed,' said Dodge. 'And that stench, my friend, is the smell of freedom.' He inhaled deeply and gave Ollie a grin. 'Now, are you coming or not?'

Ollie looked again at the manhole, and saw Dodge had already disappeared down the ladder inside. Taking a deep breath, and with one last glance at the early morning sky, Ollie followed him into the darkness.

3 SECRET CITY

It was like descending into a different world. The air was cool, damp and utterly still. Once Ollie had slid the manhole cover back into place, the only light came from the torch on Dodge's phone.

Ollie followed Dodge down the ladder, the rungs greasy in his grip.

'Easy now,' said Dodge. 'Almost there. Two more rungs . . . that's it. Watch your step when you reach the bottom.'

Ollie dropped down beside Dodge. He landed feet first in a puddle of water. It wasn't sewage water, he didn't think. More likely rain water that had dripped through the shaft they'd just descended. Even so it wasn't exactly pleasant and Ollie curled his toes at the cold.

'You could do with some shoes,' Dodge said, pointing out the obvious. 'And those PJs . . .' He shone the torch on Ollie's midriff. 'Don't get me wrong, I like dinosaurs as much as the next man, but don't you reckon you should've bought the next size up?'

Ollie looked down and almost curdled with embarrassment. He was still wearing his dino pyjamas, which was bad enough, but he'd got them for his birthday more than two years ago, and he'd long outgrown them. The sleeves barely covered his wrists, and the trousers ended above his ankles. Dodge, in contrast, wore combats, a Nike T-shirt and scuffed-up chequerboard Vans.

'Hey,' said Dodge, clearly sensing Ollie's discomfort. 'It's no big deal. All the toughest guys wear pyjamas. Karate experts, ninjas and . . . er . . . convicts. And besides, we can kit you out with something more appropriate when we get home.'

Dodge turned and started trotting along the tunnel, splashing through puddles as he went. They were on a walkway of some sort, the sewage itself forming an underground river alongside them.

Dodge was tapping into his phone again, sending another message, Ollie guessed.

'Does that work down here? How have you even got a signal?'

Dodge threw a grin across his shoulder. 'A friend of mine made a few modifications. Short-wave antenna, a bespoke messaging app and our own private frequency.' He waggled the phone in Ollie's direction and Ollie glimpsed that funny aerial thing he'd noticed before. 'It doesn't look pretty, but it works great. Jack's a genius. I'll introduce you when we get home.'

That reference to *home* again. Where on earth could he mean? Ollie was pretty sure it wasn't a cosy three-bed semi in the suburbs, nor a flat like the one he and Nancy had shared in Chalk Farm.

Nancy.

Ollie felt her absence in his stomach, a sudden jolt like a physical blow. She was gone. Their life together, gone. It was as though the floor beneath his feet had collapsed from under him, and he had no means of knowing where he would land.

'This way,' Dodge said, bearing left. He fiddled with his phone and when he held it out in front of him the beam from the torch was so bright Ollie could see an extra ten, twenty metres further on. The entire circumference of the tunnel was illuminated, revealing the ancient arch of brickwork in all its slime-covered glory.

'Another modification,' Dodge explained, indicating his phone. 'High-power beam. It's murder on the battery, but as useful in its way as the aerial. These tunnels are how we get around, you see. The sewers, old railway cuttings, disused Underground ventilation channels. Sometimes even the Tube tunnels themselves. All great for accessing where we need to go, but whoever built them neglected to put in strip lights and wi-fi. Most inconsiderate, if you ask me.'

'You keep saying "we",' Ollie replied. 'Who are you talking about? And why don't you use the pavement like everyone else?'

Dodge laughed. 'We're not like everyone else, that's why. We're kids like you, Ollie. Exactly like you, in fact. And as for the tunnels . . . they're how we get where we're going without being seen. Which can be crucial in our line of work.'

'Work? But . . . how old are you? Shouldn't you be at school?'

'I'm fifteen. And the "work" thing, it's a figure of speech. I go to school. We all do. Just not the same sort of school you go to.'

Ollie was about to ask what Dodge meant when they turned another corner and hit a stench so overwhelming it was like running into a wall.

'Whoa,' Ollie gasped, tears budding in his eyes. He held his nose, and when he spoke again he sounded like he was at the thick end of a cold. 'This friend of yours,' he said to Dodge. 'Couldn't he have invented, like, some decent nose plugs or something while he was at it?'

'Jack's a *she*, not a *he*. And nose plugs would make it kind of difficult to breathe,' Dodge pointed out. 'Some of the other kids use Vicks. You know, that stuff you put on your chest when you get ill? A little dab under each nostril and the smell of the sewage isn't so bad. Me, I don't tend to bother. You get used to the pong after a while.'

Ollie wasn't sure it was something he could ever to get used to.

'And you know what?' Dodge went on. 'I'd take a sewer over the other types of tunnels down here any day. They're roomier for starters. Some of those London Underground ventilation tunnels, you'd think they were built for baby hobbits.'

Ollie would hardly have described the sewer they were moving through as roomy.

'As for the Tube tunnels themselves,' Dodge was saying, 'there's the whole getting-splattered-by-a-passing-train thing I'm basically happy to do without. So yeah, on the whole the sewers are our friends.'

Ollie trod in something then that definitely *wasn't* friendly. His PJ bottoms were clinging wetly to his calves, so that the cold reached almost to his knees.

'I still think I'd rather go by pavement,' he grumbled.

'Ha.' Dodge glanced back at him with another grin. 'Just you wait,' he said. 'I guarantee you'll change your tune soon enough. Above us, right now? That's the Tower of London. A few more corners and we'll be under the Bank of England.'

'The Bank of England?'

Dodge smiled. 'See? I knew you'd be impressed. The world down here? It's like a secret city. One nobody knows about except us.'

That *was* pretty cool, Ollie had to admit.

'The only thing you really need to worry about is the rats.'

Ollie turned. 'Rats?'

'Can't you hear them?'

Ollie listened and found that he could. Little scurrying noises along the channel below them. A squeak now and then, too. He tried to peer over to see if he could spot them, but he was distracted by the sight of lights dancing in the tunnel up ahead.

'Relax,' Dodge said, when Ollie stiffened. 'Those men back there will be searching for us in their yard. These guys, they're with me. Oh, and that reminds me. Give me your hand.'

'What?' Ollie said.

'Your hand. Hold it out.'

'But . . . why?' Ollie asked, even as he offered Dodge his palm.

'Safety measures,' Dodge responded, and before Ollie knew what was happening, Dodge had spun him round and got him in an arm lock.

'Hey!'

'Sorry to have to do this to you, Ollie.'

Ollie wriggled, but it did no good. Dodge drove him against the slimy sewer wall. Ollie caught a flash of black fabric, and then all of a sudden the world went dark. After that he felt his free arm being wrenched behind him, and something dig painfully into his wrists. For the second time in twelve hours, Ollie found himself a prisoner, his head hooded and his hands firmly fastened behind his back.

4 SEWER RUN

Whoever was up ahead was drawing closer. Ollie could no longer see the lights, but he could hear footsteps in the shallow standing water. It was hard to tell how many people were arriving. Two, at least, Ollie would have said, though perhaps as many as four.

Dodge was walking with Ollie in front of him, guiding him with a hand around the back of his neck. So much for his new friend. So much for being rescued. He should have dropped on top of Dodge when he'd had the opportunity, or taken his chances with that barbed-wire fence.

Ollie was tempted to try to swing a heel into his captor's shins, but he had a sense Dodge would be half expecting it. And besides, even if Ollie did get away, he would still be hooded and bound. Dodge's friends would surely recapture him in an instant.

'Easy now,' Dodge said, pulling Ollie to a standstill.

'Hey, Dodge,' said an approaching voice. A girl's. 'Where's this "package" you've been texting us about? I can't . . . Oh.'

The girl must have caught sight of Ollie in Dodge's shadow. Once again he thought about how ridiculous he must look. Not only barefoot and in little kids' PJs, but with a pillowcase over his head.

'What have you been up to, Dodge? Snatching little kids from their beds?' A boy's voice this time: deeper, meaner. 'This isn't *The BFG*, you know.'

Slowly Ollie started backing away, hoping no one would notice. His hands were fastened tight, but the hood was loose, meaning if he tipped his head forwards and shook, he might be able to get it off.

Just as he thought he'd gained enough distance to try to make a break for it, he felt the familiar clasp of Dodge's hand around his neck.

This time Ollie bucked. 'Get off me,' he said.

'What do you know? It speaks!' The boy again. 'What's with the get-up, kid? Are you, like, doing something for charity? The Barefoot Tiny Pyjamas Sewer Run. Put me down for fifty pence a mile.'

'Shut up,' Ollie responded, wriggling. 'And don't call me "kid".'

'That's enough,' said Dodge, and Ollie wasn't sure if he was talking to him or to his bully friend. 'Sol? Lily? Grab an arm each, would you? Flea, you take point. I'll bring up the rear.'

'Sure thing, boss.' This time it was a voice Ollie hadn't heard yet. Another boy's: kinder and not as deep. There were three of them in total, Ollie figured, not counting him and Dodge. Two boys, Sol and Flea, and one girl, Lily.

26

'Wait,' said the boy with the deeper voice, the one who'd spoken before. 'We're taking him with us?'

'That's right,' Dodge answered.

'No way. Not gonna happen, Dodge.'

'It's what we do, Flea. It's what we've always done.'

'But things have changed. You're the one who keeps saying that to us.'

'Sure, but . . . this is different. I've got a feeling.'

'A *feeling*?' Flea mocked. 'Oh well, that's all right then. You know. If you've got a *feeling*.'

'Shut up, Flea,' said the girl. Lily. She was talking from right beside Ollie's ear, and he felt her take hold of his arm.

Ollie's other arm was seized, too, by Sol, Ollie presumed.

'Let me go,' Ollie said. 'I don't *want* to go with you. Just leave me here.'

'You see?' said Flea. 'Pyjama Party here doesn't even want to come. Let's ditch him and focus on the mission.'

Lily tutted. Ollie could practically hear her rolling her eyes.

'Stop whining and get on point, Flea,' Dodge said. A hand fell on Ollie's shoulder. 'And I'm sorry, Ollie. But I'm afraid you've already seen too much.'

They walked in silence after that through the sewer. At first Ollie refused to walk, but then Sol spoke softly in his ear.

'It's Ollie, right?' he said. 'Well, relax, Ollie. If you fight we're going to have to drag you, and from the look of you you're already damp enough. Besides, the blindfold is just a precaution, for our sakes as much as yours.'

It was an echo of what Dodge had said before he'd spun Ollie into an arm lock. 'Safety measures' was the phrase he'd used, and in spite of himself Ollie was curious about where they were taking him – what it was they were so eager to protect.

When they finally came to a halt, the hood was whipped off Ollie's head. He blinked, and found himself staring at a wall. Dodge freed his wrists, and Ollie rubbed at the marks that had been left by the rope.

They were in a narrow offshoot of the tunnel they'd been walking along. It was still dark, but with the walls so close together here the glow from Dodge's phone was all the brighter.

Dodge himself was at Ollie's shoulder. The others were gathered behind, but Dodge pointed at the wall before Ollie could turn.

'Look here,' he instructed.

Ollie glowered. 'Why should I do anything you say?'

Dodge sighed. 'Look, Ollie. I'm sorry about the dramatics. But you'll understand soon enough why they were necessary. You're not hurt, are you? And we got you away from those men, didn't we?'

Grudgingly, Ollie turned, but as far as he could tell Dodge was pointing at a brick.

'*Here*,' Dodge said, moving his finger closer.

Ollie saw a small, circular lens hidden in the brickwork.

'Is that a camera?' he said.

'Say "cheese",' Dodge answered.

Ollie just blinked.

'Facial recognition,' Dodge explained. 'And now, put your thumb on here.' There was another small, dark circle in the brickwork, lower down this time, but again so well concealed Ollie would never have spotted it if it hadn't been pointed out to him.

When Ollie hesitated, Dodge took hold of his hand and pressed his thumb to the sensor plate for him.

'Fingerprint recognition,' he said. 'It's nothing fancy – basically the tech from an iPhone 5S. Pretty cool, though, huh? And now you're on our system.'

Ollie heard a dissatisfied grunt behind him. Flea, he assumed, but as Ollie was about to look back at him, Dodge pressed his own thumb to the reader and the wall in front of them cracked open.

It wasn't a wall at all, Ollie realised, but a door, camouflaged to look like its surroundings.

Dodge stepped aside to reveal a narrow flight of steps leading up. He gestured for Ollie to lead the way.

*   *   *

The first thing Ollie noticed was the smell. After the sewage, it was as pleasurable as walking into a bakery. Except, instead of bread, the odour reminded him of . . . books. That smell when you open the pages of a novel and press your nose right up against the spine.

'Keep going,' said Dodge from behind him. 'All the way up.'

The room at the top of the stairs looked very much like one of the changing rooms at Ollie's school. There were benches around the perimeter, hooks on the walls, and in the furthest corner a row of lockers. On the ceiling was a flickering row of strip lights.

'This is the kit room,' Dodge said, and as Ollie lingered in the doorway, the others squeezed by him. All except one of them; the last person through deliberately bumped Ollie's shoulder.

'Whoops. Sorry, kid.'

Ollie recognised the voice of Flea, and for the first time Ollie was able to get a look at him. He was tall, taller than Dodge even, and probably about the same age. Whereas Dodge was fair, however, Flea had dark hair and dark eyes. His neck was so thick it appeared to be almost wider than his head.

Flea peeled off the sweatshirt he was wearing, revealing his broad shoulders and muscled arms. He wasn't someone you wanted as an enemy, clearly, but Ollie was already coming to think of him as exactly that.

'Here, Ollie. These should fit.'

Ollie turned just in time to catch a bundle of clothes Dodge had tossed towards him. Some navy combats like the ones Dodge was wearing, a plain white T-shirt and a soft, grey hooded sweatshirt.

'There should be some trainers in the corner as well. Just pick a pair that fit.'

Ollie moved hesitantly towards the stack of shoes Dodge had indicated. He was about to slip off his damp pyjamas when he remembered who else was in the room.

He turned, and saw Lily watching him from beside the lockers. She blushed and looked away, but not before Ollie caught a glimpse of her fawn eyes and pale skin.

'This way, Ollie,' said a voice beside him. Sol was slightly younger, Ollie thought, though still older than Ollie. He had dark skin and short, hedgehog-y dreadlocks, and a glint in his broad, bright eyes. 'There's a bathroom through that door in the corner,' Sol went on. 'You . . . er . . . might want to wash your feet.'

Ollie looked down. His feet weren't just dirty, they were black. And there was . . . stuff sticking out from between his toes. Ollie didn't want to contemplate what it might be.

'Thanks,' he mumbled, and with another quick glance at Lily, padded off towards the bathroom.

The clothes were slightly too big in the end, but Ollie wasn't about to complain. He liked his hoodies baggy anyway, and the trousers he could simply roll up. From the stack of trainers he'd found a pair of Adidas shelltoes – white with red stripes – that were cool in a retro sort of way.

Once he was changed he checked himself in the mirror, wiping the grime from his cheeks and doing his best to flatten down his shock of copper-blond hair. He gave up in the end. Normally the only thing that worked was high-strength gel and even at home Ollie could rarely be bothered.

He drank deeply from the tap, not minding the taste of warm metal, then headed back into the kit room.

'Better,' said Dodge, approvingly, and Ollie noticed Sol and Lily smile.

Flea grunted. 'You'll always be "PJ" to me, kid,' he said, and he turned and headed towards the exit. There was no door this time, just another set of stairs leading up.

'Don't mind him,' Sol said to Ollie conspiratorially. 'The doctor dropped him when he was a baby. If you look him straight in the eyes you can see the squint.' He crossed his eyes then, sticking out his tongue and tilting his head, and for the first time since all of this had begun, Ollie found himself smiling.

He followed Sol and the others where Flea had led, the smell of books intensifying as they climbed. The stairs where they'd first entered were made of steel, and seemed to have been installed relatively recently. This staircase was stone, and some of the steps were worn so badly they were barely steps at all.

They emerged a moment later into a corridor, and although there were no windows, there were misted skylights overhead, and Ollie could tell they'd reached ground level.

They headed along the passageway, which Ollie had the impression was a link to another building. Flea was leading and Dodge was bringing up the rear. At the door at the far end, Flea paused. This time there was a camera in plain view, plus a panel at waist height that might well have housed a fingerprint sensor. Flea didn't use them, though. Instead he looked back along the corridor, and for a second when he spoke Ollie thought Flea was talking to him.

'Last chance. You sure you want to do this?'

Do what? Ollie was about to say, when he heard Dodge answer from across his shoulder.

'It's already done, Flea. Now, let's introduce Ollie to his new home.'

5 CONTROL ROOM

'What *is* this place?'

Ollie's first thought when they stepped inside was that they'd entered a church. No, not a church, a cathedral, so grand was the central hall.

There were no religious pictures on the walls, however, and no crosses or anything like that. The windows were high up, but they weren't stained glass. Instead they were a plain frosted white, like the skylights in the walkway they'd just come through. And whereas every church Ollie had ever entered funnelled towards the raised platform at the front, this building seemed to sprawl in every direction. There were corridors leading off like spokes, though Ollie couldn't see where they led.

'This place,' said Dodge, casting his eyes at the domed ceiling. The hall was three storeys high, rising up through the building like a central hub. 'This is where we live. Beautiful, isn't it? If a little past its best.' As if to demonstrate his point, he reached towards the nearest wall and pulled off a bit of old plaster. It came away easily, and a mist of dust puffed and settled on the floor. 'We'll give you the full tour later. There's lots to see.

But for the moment let's go to the control room, and we can all introduce ourselves properly.'

The control room?

Ollie followed where Dodge led: across the mosaic floor and up the sweeping central staircase. The others trailed in their wake. As they walked Ollie noticed how noisy the building was. Not football-stadium noisy. More like a supermarket or a shopping centre or something. People were talking somewhere just out of sight. Behind the doors along those corridors, Ollie assumed. And the voices he heard . . . if Ollie didn't know better, he would have said they all belonged to *kids*.

'A word of advice,' said Dodge as they climbed. 'Be a bit careful where you step. This staircase is fine.' He patted the thick oak handrail. 'Wood like this, it will probably be standing a thousand years from now. But elsewhere around the building . . . She's a little past her best, as I said. A lot of the floorboards are rotten, and probably quite a few of the beams. The top floor, the third, is in the worst state. We tend to avoid going up there if we can.'

They reached the first floor, which had the same spoke-like system of corridors as the ground floor, and a balcony that looked down on the central hallway. Ollie moved to peer over, but Dodge hauled him back.

'And I wouldn't trust those bannisters if I were you.' He gave the handrail on the mezzanine a wobble. 'Not unless you're feeling brave.'

Flea, Lily and Sol had continued past them, and Ollie saw Flea grab Lily's shoulders and pretend to push her over.

'Mind you don't trip,' he said, and laughed.

Lily barely reacted. It was almost as though she'd been expecting it – as though Flea had tried that joke a zillion times before. She elbowed him in the bicep.

'You're an idiot, Fletcher Hunter.'

'So you keep telling me,' Flea answered, still grinning.

'Well, maybe one day it'll penetrate that thick skull of yours.'

Ollie caught Dodge rolling his eyes. 'Honestly,' he said. 'I always thought twins were supposed to get along.'

'Twins?' Ollie replied. 'What do you mean?'

'They're not identical, obviously. In fact there's hardly any resemblance at all. But Lily and Flea? They're brother and sister. In fact it was Lily who gave Flea his nickname. Said it was perfect for him because he was so irritating. Flea thought it was cool because fleas are, like, super strong. Apparently.' Dodge saw Ollie's face and smiled. 'You look shocked.'

'No, I . . . Well. Maybe a bit.'

Dodge looked pleased. 'Better get used to it, Ollie,' he said. 'You'll find we're full of surprises.'

They followed the others into a room lined with computers, like in one of the ICT labs in Ollie's school. There were seven or eight monitors at intervals along a wall-length desk, and an assortment of chairs facing each one. They were proper computer chairs, the type you saw in offices, but every one of them appeared to be broken in some way. Most had at least one arm missing, and all the cushions were worn and ripped.

The computer equipment had seen better days, too. There was enough of it, and from the flash of lights and the hum of hard drives, it all appeared to be working well enough, but even the computers in Ollie's school were newer. And everything was plugged into a dangerous-looking tangle of extension leads, sprouting from a single power point on the wall. Mr Hutchinson, his ICT teacher at school, would probably have had a heart attack.

On two of the computer screens there were images from the security cameras they'd passed, plus a number they hadn't. There was a view of roofs, and Ollie recognised some of the buildings in the distance. The Gherkin, St Paul's, even Tower Bridge.

'The control room', Dodge had called this place, but it was more like a security centre, Ollie thought. He wondered again what it was these kids were so secretive about that they needed a full-on security system to guard it.

'Ollie? This is Jack. The genius I mentioned before.'

Ollie looked across and saw a girl with freckles and short, spiky, ginger hair. She moved out from behind her desk in the corner of the room and Ollie realised she was in a wheelchair.

'A genius, he says,' muttered Jack. 'As though it matters how high my IQ is when I've got a budget as low as the one they give me here.' She propelled her wheelchair across the room, and would have rolled right across Ollie's new trainers if he hadn't leapt backwards in time. 'Pleasure,' she grumbled as she passed him, in a tone that suggested she struggled to find much pleasure in anything, least of all interacting with a stranger.

'Don't take it personally,' Dodge whispered once Jack had settled behind another desk. 'She's like that even when you get to know her. She's more a computer person than a people person, if you know what I mean.'

'I heard that,' Jack responded, without shifting her eyes from her monitor. 'I'm telling you, Dodge, if it wasn't so difficult for me to get around this place, I would already be rolling out the door. And I'm not the only one here with mobility issues. Where's that stairlift you keep promising us?'

Flea stepped forwards and flexed his arms, posing like a circus strongman. 'Right here, baby,' he said. 'Make my phone do everything Dodge's does, and I'll carry you wherever you want to go.'

It was hard to tell because she had her back to them, but Ollie would have sworn Jack gave a smile. The others smiled, too, even Lily. Looking at her and Flea side by side, Ollie still wouldn't have guessed they were related, let alone twins.

Whereas Flea was all bulges and angles, Lily's appearance was altogether softer, right down to the subtle colour of her eyes.

Ollie had never paid much attention to girls. He'd seen with his mates at school how complicated friendships suddenly became once girlfriends entered the equation. There was no denying that Lily was pretty, however. More importantly, she seemed smart, as well as funny.

Dodge pulled Ollie further into the room. It was L-shaped, and bigger than Ollie had first realised.

Around the corner were more computers – as old as the others – and a table that was stacked with what looked like maps, some spread out on the surface, others curled into rolls. There were whiteboards, pinboards, even a blackboard, and all were filled with images, diagrams, newspaper articles, handwritten notes, you name it. There was obviously a system of some kind to the way the information was laid out, but at first glance Ollie couldn't tell what it might be. It was like being in some mad scientist's inventing lab.

There were two other people in the room. Both kids, like the others, and again Ollie's age or slightly older.

Dodge pointed to the boy who was working in the corner. He had blond hair and round, frameless glasses, which were balanced at the tip of his nose. 'Over there, that's Erik. He's our linguist.'

'Your what?'

'Our languages guy. Say hello, Erik.'

'Hello, Erik,' said Erik. It was hard to tell from the two words he'd uttered, but it sounded as if he had an accent of some kind. German, maybe? Scandinavian?

'And over there,' Dodge went on, 'that's Song. If Jack's our genius when it comes to computers, Song's our go-to girl on all things maths.'

Maths? Ollie found himself thinking, and Dodge clocked his reaction.

'Don't knock it,' he said. 'Secret codes, data encryption, even safe cracking – you'd be amazed how many problems mathematics can solve.'

The girl, Song, waved cheerfully, then got back to whatever she was doing.

'And that's us, basically,' Dodge said, spreading his arms. 'Sol, Flea and Lily you've already met, even if you haven't been formally introduced. There are others, too, who contribute when their particular skills are needed, but the people in this room are pretty much the core team.'

Ollie glanced at everyone around him. It was almost too much for him to take in: too many names, too many faces, too much he didn't understand. He focused on Dodge, who was clearly the leader.

'But . . . what sort of team?' he said. 'Who *are* you guys?'

Dodge and the others exchanged glances. The kids from the tunnel – Sol, Lily and Flea – were close beside him. The rest of

41

the team – Jack, Erik and Song – were still at their various workstations.

'We don't exactly have a name,' Dodge said. 'But this place . . . we call it the Haven. And our little group here – we're the investigations wing.'

Flea scoffed. 'The "investigations wing",' he muttered derisively.

'The Haven?' Ollie echoed, focusing on Dodge. 'But . . . what do you do here? And why all the secrecy? The cameras, the blindfold, all that.'

'We do plenty. Too much, it feels like sometimes,' Dodge added, with a meaningful glance at Flea. 'But essentially, we help kids.'

'Kids? What type of kids?'

'Any kids. All kids. Kids who need us. Kids who have nowhere else to go.'

'Like . . . homeless kids, you mean?'

'Homeless kids, sure. Refugees. Orphans. Kids who get caught up with gangs. The queen's granddaughter if she needed us. We're really not fussy.'

'And you're in charge? What about the adults? Where are they?'

Dodge grinned. 'That's the coolest part. There aren't any.'

'What do you mean?'

'Just what I say. There aren't any. When this place was first established, there weren't any adults around anyway. And since then, well. We've come to realise that grown-ups don't always have kids' interests at heart.'

There was a murmur of agreement from the rest of the group.

'But *we* do, Ollie,' Dodge went on. 'Kids' interests, their welfare – that's *all* we care about. You could call it our guiding principle. It's why the Haven was set up in the first place.'

'But . . . I still don't understand what it is you—'

'Look,' Flea cut in, 'I hate to interrupt this little life lesson, Dodge, but when are you going to get to the part where you tell us what you found?'

'Yeah, Dodge,' said Lily. 'Did you see anything? Were there any leads?'

The group had closed around Dodge, eager to hear what he had to say, and Ollie found himself shoulder to shoulder with Sol.

'What are they talking about?' Ollie whispered. 'What leads?'

Sol kept his eyes on Dodge as he leant closer to Ollie and whispered back, 'Some kids have been going missing. Not rich kids, though. Strays like us, meaning the police haven't done a thing about it. Dodge went to the warehouse because we had a lead. Flea did.' Something seemed to occur to Sol then, and he turned to face Ollie fully. 'Say. That's where he found you, right? Dodge? Is that where you found Ollie? So what Flea heard – is it true?'

Dodge broke off from whatever he'd been saying to the others. 'Ollie has nothing to do with this. He was with a cop. Your friend, you said – right, Ollie? Meaning your guardian or something?'

It was all Ollie could do to bring himself to nod. He felt the others watching him intently – Lily in particular – and there came that familiar prickle behind his eyes.

Dodge spoke up to rescue him.

'Look,' he said. 'The warehouse was a washout. That's what it boils down to. Sorry, Flea, but that lead you had? It didn't come through.'

Flea looked furious. 'That little weasel. He swore blind he saw kids being taken into that building.'

'Who's he talking about?' Ollie asked Sol.

'His source, I imagine,' Sol answered. 'The kid who gave him the lead in the first place. A runaway. Someone Flea found sleeping on the streets.'

'Two months I've been bringing him food,' Flea was saying. 'He would have starved if it wasn't for me. And how does he repay me? By sending us all off on a wild goose chase!'

'You should have brought him here,' said Lily. 'After two months sleeping in a doorway, he was probably desperate. He would have said anything to get you to keep helping him.'

'I would have, wouldn't I?' snapped Flea. 'But Dodge says we're full, that there's no room at the inn.'

'We are full, Flea!' said Dodge. 'Look around you. Look at the state of this place. We're going through a bit of a funding crisis, in case you hadn't noticed.'

'Oh yeah? So what's with PJ here? Why is *he* the exception?'

All eyes turned towards Ollie. He doubted he could have felt smaller. 'I didn't *want* to come here, remember?' he said. 'And anyway, I've no intention of staying.'

'Well, that's one bit of good news at least,' said Flea. 'Tell me when you want to leave and I'll show you the door.'

'Right now would be fine by me,' said Ollie, aware his grief at what had happened to Nancy was turning into anger. 'And you can keep your stupid clothes, too. I'd rather walk across London in my pyjamas than stay here another minute with the likes of you.'

'Easy now,' said Dodge, moving between them. 'Ollie's here at my invitation. I've got a sense he might be able to contribute.'

Flea was about to answer back, but Dodge cut him off with a look.

'So what next, Dodge?' Sol seemed eager to defuse the tension. 'If Maddy Sikes had nothing to do with this, where do you think we should look next? That's six kids this week. All gang members. All from different parts of the city.'

Ollie and Flea had been glaring at each other over Dodge's shoulder, but at the mention of Maddy Sikes, Ollie broke eye contact. Dodge had spoken about Maddy Sikes back in the warehouse. Was she the person responsible for Nancy's murder?

'Seven kids,' chipped in Erik, who didn't shift his eyes from his computer screen. 'We had word while you were gone. One of Danny Hunter's crew disappeared last night.'

'Danny Hunter?' echoed Lily. 'Oh, that's just great. First the Diamonds, then the Shiver Street Posse, and now the Razors.'

'Gang names,' Sol whispered to Ollie. 'They're not exactly friends of ours, any of them.'

Dodge was thinking. He ran a knuckle along the length of his scar. 'Well,' he said at last, 'there's your answer. You asked what next, Sol. As far as I can see, we don't have an option.'

Sol swallowed. 'You don't mean . . .'

Dodge nodded. 'We speak to Danny.' He laid a hand on Ollie's shoulder. 'And if you really want to know what it is we do here, Ollie, this is your chance to find out.'

6 MAD MADDY

Maddy Sikes sat staring at her computer screen, enjoying the final moments of Detective Inspector Nancy Bedwin's life.

She watched the footage over and over, playing it from the moment her two guards walked into the room, to the point just after the bullets they fired bloomed in Nancy's chest.

As deaths went it wasn't the most elaborate, but there was an attractiveness about its brutal efficiency.

Sikes would have liked to have killed Nancy herself, as payback for all the inconvenience she and her investigation had caused. But Sikes *had* killed her, really. She'd given the order, and that was what counted, not who'd actually pulled the trigger.

So, ninety-nine.

That was Sikes's running tally, the number of lives in her personal collection. Not all had been captured on CCTV, of course, which was another reason Nancy's death was so precious.

But ninety-nine was the total. It was a reasonable figure. A respectable one. Yet if everything Sikes was plotting went as planned, it would very quickly leap an awful lot higher. An *awful* lot.

Sikes eased backwards in her chair, her faithful dog, Bullseye, at her feet. Behind her, the London skyline was framed by the enormous floor-to-ceiling windows of her office. The view was one of the finest in the city, and was part of the reason Sikes had chosen to locate her headquarters up here on the fifty-first floor of the skyscraper she owned from the basement up. Sikes had spent many hours gazing out, surveying her would-be empire below. For the time being, though, her attention was on the images playing out in front of her.

She rewound the footage and watched it again. Once Nancy lay dead on the floor, Sikes allowed the video to carry on playing. It had been spliced together with a clip of the boy running through the corridor, and Sikes took a moment to enjoy his obvious, unadulterated panic.

Ollie Turner.

That was the boy's name, apparently.

Turner. Turner. Why did that surname ring bells?

It was common enough, Sikes supposed. Probably she'd had a teacher called Turner in that awful boarding school her parents had forced her to attend – an experience years of hypnotherapy had failed to wipe from her mind.

Sikes rewound the footage, and was midway through watching it again when there was a knuckle tap at her office door. Bullseye raised his head and growled, as though attuned to Sikes's annoyance at the interruption.

'Easy, Bullseye,' said Sikes, and she reached to scratch behind Bullseye's ear with one of her claw-like fingernails.

Sikes was aware of the theory that dogs tended to resemble their owners, and she knew that she and Bullseye were a case in point. Bullseye was a Siberian husky, a breed whose elegant appearance belied its pitiless nature, which could certainly have been said of Sikes herself. The dog's hair, like Sikes's, was pure white, and around his neck he wore a collar encrusted with diamonds, especially commissioned to replicate Sikes's priceless watch. And when Bullseye snarled, there was a savagery to his expression that bore an uncanny resemblance to Sikes when she smiled.

'Enter.'

Sikes's assistant, Grimwig, poked his head into the room. He was a short man with an unfortunate face. He looked almost shark-like, with his sharp, pointy little teeth and his eyes set so far towards the outside of his head. His brain, though, was as finely honed as a carving knife.

'Your guest is here, Ms Sikes,' he said. 'Right on schedule.'

Sikes nodded. 'Show him what he needs to see. Ensure he gets straight to work.'

Grimwig gave something like a bow. He was about to leave when Sikes spoke again.

'The policewoman. Have you disposed of her body?'

'In the usual manner, Ms Sikes.'

Meaning Nancy Bedwin's final act had been to take a bath in the river Thames.

Sikes smiled, and dismissed Grimwig with a flick of her fingers. Her assistant slid from the room and closed the door noiselessly behind him.

Sikes reached again and tickled Bullseye's ears. The shipment was taken care of, the doctor had been smuggled into the country to oversee the final preparations, and Nancy Bedwin was out of the picture. It was all coming together nicely.

And there was young Ollie Turner, of course, captured in a frozen frame on Sikes's computer screen. A missed opportunity, she'd thought before. But maybe there was still a chance that Ollie Turner would become her one hundredth victim. It would be a pleasing artistic flourish, and a suitable prelude to the unveiling of Maddy Sikes's greatest masterwork of all.

7 DANNY'S RAZORS

They were back in the tunnels. Ollie was blindfolded by a hood again, and Sol was his guide. It was the same crew as before: Dodge, Sol, Lily and Flea, though this time Erik had also come along. Strength in numbers, Dodge had said, although none of the others had seemed particularly reassured. They were heading north-west, towards the part of the city controlled by Danny Hunter and his Razors.

Danny was in his early fifties, Dodge had explained, and had been head of the Razors since his seventeenth birthday. They'd been called the Panthers before that day, run by Danny's father, and it was because of the way Danny had chosen to use his father's razor that had both ensured the change of leadership and won the gang their new name. Since then every member of Danny's gang had carried a cutthroat razor in their pocket, and not because they enjoyed a close shave.

The more Ollie heard about Danny Hunter, the happier he was he would never have to meet him. Ollie had decided to go with Dodge and the others on the journey, but he intended to go his separate way once they'd got to Camden. The Haven was somewhere in the east of the city, from what he'd gathered, which meant Camden was on his route home anyway.

He'd meant what he'd said to Flea, even though he'd spoken in anger. He didn't want to stay at the Haven. More importantly, he couldn't. He had to tell the police what had happened to Nancy. And Ollie had a lead for them. A name.

Maddy Sikes.

If Sikes was as big a deal in the criminal underworld as Dodge and the others had made her sound, Nancy's colleagues would probably already know all about her. And once they connected Sikes to Nancy's death, it would surely only be a matter of time before Sikes herself was brought to justice.

Wouldn't it?

Ollie felt Sol guide him around a corner, and from the smell Ollie could tell they were back in one of the sewers. Dodge was up ahead, with Flea, Lily and Erik bringing up the rear. The group behind him were having a muted conversation and Ollie couldn't help but overhear.

'I've got one,' Flea declared.

'Got one what?' Erik answered.

'A name. For us lot. You know, the *investigations* wing,' Flea said.

'We don't need a name,' Lily put in. 'Why are you so determined to invent one? We're just kids, just *us*. It's all *missions* and *tactics* and *operations* with you. If you're so determined to act like a soldier, why don't you go and join the army?'

'Like, *hello*?' said Flea to his sister. 'Look at what we're doing. Look at where we're heading. We *are* soldiers, in case you hadn't noticed. And every military unit has to have a name. It's one of the things that helps inspire fear.'

'*Fear?* We're here to help people, remember? Why would we want to inspire *fear*?'

'Just . . . in case. Wouldn't you feel better walking into Danny Hunter's territory knowing his lot were as scared of us as we are of them?'

Lily clucked then, as though she were comforting a little kid. 'Aw. I didn't realise you were *scared*, little brother. Would you like your big sister to hold your hand?'

Sol and Erik laughed. Even Ollie couldn't help smiling beneath his hood.

'Hey. Keep it down back there.'

At Dodge's reprimand the laughter dwindled.

'Eight minutes, sis,' mumbled Flea. 'That's how much older than me you are. Eight poxy minutes.'

'And yet it feels like eight years,' Lily retorted. 'Although they do always say that girls mature faster than boys.'

Sol and Erik chuckled, more quietly this time so as not to draw Dodge's ire.

'So?' said Sol, after a pause. 'What's this name you've come up with, Flea?'

'Not telling you,' said Flea, grumpily.

This time Lily was the one to laugh.

'What?' demanded Flea. 'What's the point if none of you even cares?'

'Don't be like that,' said Sol. '*We* care. Don't we, Erik?'

'Sure,' said Erik, clearly doing his best to sound sincere. 'Come on, Flea. Tell us. We promise we won't laugh.'

'I don't,' said Lily. 'Just for the record.'

Flea ignored her. 'You ready?' he said. 'You're gonna love this, I guarantee you.' He left a pause, like a silent drum roll. 'We're . . . the Shadow Puppets,' he announced, in what was obviously his best movie-trailer voice.

As one they came to a standstill . . . and Sol, Erik and Lily cracked up. Lily was laughing so hard she kept making this little squeaking noise through her nose.

'*The Shadow Puppets*,' she echoed. She tried to say more, but couldn't.

'What?' Flea demanded, indignant. 'What's so funny? We work in the shadows, right? And puppets . . . they're kind of creepy. So, the Shadow Puppets. It's perfect.'

There was a fresh wave of laughter. Lily was the first to recover, but only because she sounded all laughed out. It was like listening to a car on its last drops of petrol. 'You did say you wanted to inspire *fear*,' she said, 'not ridicule?'

More laughter. Ollie wasn't sure where Dodge had got to – presumably he'd pulled further ahead when Ollie and the others had come to a halt – but the renewed bout of noise brought him back in a hurry.

'What the hell are you lot playing at?' Dodge hissed. 'You know the rules when we're down here. Just because we know the inspection schedules doesn't mean we've necessarily got these tunnels to ourselves.'

The others fell immediately silent. Ollie couldn't see them, but he was pretty sure they were all bowing their heads. Dodge may only have been fifteen, yet he commanded as much authority as any adult.

'We've got a job to do, remember?' Dodge went on. 'Let's keep our minds on finding those missing kids.'

There was a chorus of muttered apologies. Ollie heard Dodge turn around and splash angrily back along the tunnel. Sol took Ollie by the arm and together they started walking.

There was quiet for a while, a bit like the silence Ollie had experienced in class after the entire form had been rollocked by the teacher. But then, just like in class, as people started to make eye contact with their friends, Ollie could sense the mood lighten.

'The Shadow Puppets,' he heard Sol mutter, and Ollie could imagine him shooting a surreptitious smile towards Lily.

Ollie smiled, too, but not at the name Flea had suggested. It was more the camaraderie he was witnessing, the depth of friendship that seemed to exist among these kids, which he'd never really experienced first-hand himself.

Five corners later, the entire group came to a halt.

'Sorry again about the blindfold, Ollie,' Dodge said, as he pulled the hood from Ollie's head. 'We don't often have visitors at the Haven. And no matter how much we trust them, we simply can't take the risk.'

Ollie blinked and rubbed his eyes, and saw they'd stopped beside a ladder leading up to another manhole cover. 'At least you didn't tie me up this time,' he said.

Dodge looked sheepish. 'Yeah, I suppose that was a bit heavy-handed. I didn't want to say so at the time, but I thought I heard someone following us along the tunnel, meaning there wasn't time to have a reasoned conversation.'

'Wait,' cut in Lily. 'Someone followed you? From the warehouse, you mean? Why didn't you say something?'

'I said I *thought* I heard someone following. Probably I was imagining things.'

Lily said nothing, but it was obvious she wasn't reassured.

'Enough chat,' said Dodge. 'The Razors are waiting, remember?'

'Let's hope they're *not* waiting,' said Sol, grimly.

They climbed the ladder and clambered out into the midday sun. Dodge threw each of them an energy bar, and Ollie gobbled his down. It was the first thing he'd had to eat since he'd had dinner with Nancy the previous evening.

They'd emerged close to a canal, and Dodge led them down a slope and along the towpath. The canal was pretty enough, with the sun glinting off the surface and the overhanging trees draping their branches towards the water, but it smelt almost as bad as the sewer.

'We wouldn't normally have come above ground so early,' Dodge said, 'but if you're really intent on leaving us, Ollie, our paths don't coincide for much longer. There's a junction you can take half a kilometre ahead. Assuming you're sure, that is?'

Ollie's eyes flicked towards Lily. 'I'm sure,' he answered. He was grateful to Dodge and the others for what they'd done for him, and he wished them luck, but Ollie had his own battle to fight.

They fell into formation. Almost out of habit now, Ollie found himself walking next to Sol.

'You should stay,' Sol said to him. 'Dodge was right, what he said before. I reckon you'd fit in nicely.'

Ollie smiled, grateful, but he couldn't help throwing a glance towards Flea.

'Pay no attention to old Fleabag over there,' Sol said. 'He'd find some reason to dislike you if you were made of chocolate and topped with marshmallows. That's just his way.'

'Thanks,' Ollie said. He and Sol had been passing around a stone – kicking it between each other as though it were a football – and Ollie toed it into the water. 'But . . . Nancy,' he said. 'I need to find out what happened to Nancy.'

'Your friend, you mean?'

Ollie nodded, not quite trusting himself to speak. Sol didn't push him any further.

'Why don't they like you?' Ollie asked, a few steps later. 'The gangs, I mean. You help kids, don't you? And don't gangs have lots of kids?'

'They're *all* kids, some of them.'

'So why don't they like you?'

'For that exact reason,' Sol said.

Ollie looked at him blankly.

'You said it yourself,' Sol explained. 'The gangs in this city, especially the criminal ones, they suck in kids. Take them out of school, promise them riches and trick them into doing their dirty work. Us lot,' he said, gesturing to Dodge and the others, 'we take them back. We give them a *real* chance. Help them recover their former lives if it's not too late, otherwise take them in at the Haven. We give them food, shelter, an education. We give them a family.' Sol flushed and looked towards his feet. 'It sounds corny, I expect.'

'No, I . . . It doesn't.' It sounded the exact opposite of corny, as it happened, although Ollie wasn't sure how to put this into words. 'So they hate you for taking away their members,' he said instead. 'Is that it?'

'Basically,' Sol agreed. 'Although with Danny Hunter it goes a bit deeper than that. A lot deeper, in fact. You see, Flea and Lily—'

But he got no further. Neither he nor Ollie had been looking where they'd been going, and they walked straight into the back of Flea.

Up ahead, blocking their path, and on top of the banks either side of them, was a line of kids. Some were even younger than Ollie. Most were Dodge's age or older. They were twenty-something strong, outnumbering Dodge and the rest of them four to one. And each of them, at their side, held open a glimmering cutthroat razor.

'We were wondering whether you lot would dare to show up.'

A boy spoke down at them from the top of the bank. The sun was directly behind him, eclipsed by the set of his shoulders, so that all Ollie could really see of him was an outline. He moved, and Ollie had to recoil from the sudden glare. When he looked again the boy had slipped down on to the towpath, right into the middle of their group.

'We even had a sweepstake,' the boy went on. 'Most of the betting was against. Me, I'm gonna make a killing.' The boy grinned, and Ollie couldn't tell whether he was talking literally or metaphorically. The boy's razor gleamed at his side.

Ollie took a moment to check out the other gang members that lined the banks. Some had bikes: tatty, broken things that seemed on the verge of falling apart. Others stood forlorn in scuffed-up trainers. The thing that struck Ollie hardest was how miserable they all looked. There was none of the camaraderie he'd witnessed among the Haven kids. The thing most of the Razors seemed focused on was trying to look tough.

'Although,' the boy went on, 'I must say I'm surprised to see you here, Flea. And Dodge, didn't you learn your lesson last time? I'd have thought that scar of yours would have served as a reminder.'

Dodge's hand moved towards the scar on his cheek.

'We need to talk to Danny, Zeke. We're not here to start any trouble.'

The boy – Zeke – laughed. He was about sixteen and skinny as a pole, though Ollie had the impression he was as tough as wire. Like most of the other kids forming the perimeter around them, he wore baggy jeans and a vest top.

'Not here to start trouble,' Zeke echoed. 'And yet it always seems to kick off when you're around.'

Zeke turned to Flea. He stepped so they were almost nose to nose. 'What about you, Flea? Are you here to start trouble? This time of day, I would have thought you'd be in school.' He said this last bit mockingly, and Zeke's mates laughed. Zeke looked around to soak up the appreciation. As he did so, Flea closed the gap between them further.

'You should try it one day,' he said. 'You might learn something, like there's more to life than running around waving a piece of cutlery. You call yourself a Razor, Zeke, but all you really are is a loser, too afraid to take responsibility for your own life.'

The barb cut, clearly, and Zeke raised his blade in response. He held it level with Flea's nose, and then folded it shut with a snap.

'You say you want to see Danny,' he said. 'Well, you're in luck. Because it just so happens Danny wants to see *you*.'

8 HIGH STAKES

Zeke and the other gang members escorted them through the back streets of Camden. Eventually they stopped outside what appeared to be an abandoned theatre, like the ones near Leicester Square, but without the West-End glitz. If Zeke hadn't stopped them right outside the building, Ollie probably wouldn't have noticed it at all.

They passed through the foyer, which was too dark to allow Ollie to see properly. Once they'd funnelled into the auditorium, someone somewhere hit the lights.

It wasn't a theatre any more. The shell of the building remained in place: the curved walls, the ornate ceiling, the balcony that had once contained seating. But all the seats had been ripped out, and the stage had been levelled with the floor. In their places were an assortment of tables, green on top, and marked for the most part with various grids, lines and numbers. Ollie spotted a roulette wheel, and realised they were in a casino. An illegal one, Ollie guessed, given how from the outside it was doing its best to avoid attention.

'Like what I've done with the place?'

The Haven kids turned as one, and Ollie saw two men entering the theatre from a door beside what would once have been the stage. At first he couldn't tell which one of the men had spoken. They appeared identical. Dark suits, dark scowls and taller than Ollie would have been if he'd been standing on a chair.

But then a shorter man appeared from in between them. His suit was white, with tan leather patches on the shoulders. In place of a tie he had on one of those funny string things that cowboys wore. His belt buckle was bigger than Ollie's hand, and on his head was the type of hat Ollie had only ever seen in Westerns.

This was Danny Hunter, Ollie guessed. His bodyguards fanned out and stood to attention as Danny continued towards them. He seemed to rattle as he walked, and it took a moment for Ollie to realise that the sound was coming from something concealed in Danny's hand.

'A little slice of Nevada in old London town,' Danny said, gesturing around his casino. 'Though I hardly expect you kids to appreciate that.'

He took off his hat and tossed it on to one of the gambling tables, then sat down on one of the stools alongside it and hooked one leg over the other, revealing a pair of shiny leather cowboy boots. His hand continued to rattle.

Zeke hopped on to the roulette table and sat with his legs dangling towards the floor. He was smiling with anticipation.

Danny Hunter looked both older and younger than his fifty-something years. Younger, because his skin was unwrinkled and there wasn't a trace of grey in his swept-back hair. Older, because it was *weird* that he wasn't wrinkled and that his hair was such a solid shade of black. His face seemed set as if from a cast, and Ollie wondered if this was what happened when you had too much plastic surgery – you turned *into* plastic, basically, and started to look more like a Barbie or something. Although not a Barbie in Danny's case, obviously. More like a Cowboy Ken.

Danny raised the hand that was rattling and dropped what he was holding on to the green baize of the table. They were dice, Ollie saw. Solid gold, from the look of them.

Danny looked at what he'd rolled and smiled darkly. He gathered up the dice and started rattling them again between his fingers.

'You're in luck,' he said. 'If I'd rolled evens I would have had every one of you killed right where you're standing.'

Ollie flicked a glance to Danny's bodyguards. There were six in the room now, he counted.

'Although I'm tempted to kill you all anyway,' Danny went on. 'Even you, Lily.'

Lily moved to the head of their group. 'Hello, Uncle,' she said.

Ollie glanced at Sol. *Uncle?*

Sol gave the faintest shake of his head. *Say nothing, Ollie.*

Danny Hunter slammed his fist down on the table. Ollie couldn't help but jerk back.

'*Uncle!*' Danny roared. His rage was so ferocious that his phony features finally showed his anger. 'You lost the right to call me "uncle" a long time ago!'

Lily glanced nervously at Dodge. Ollie got the feeling that none of this was going quite according to plan.

'And as for you, Fletcher.' Danny Hunter turned his wrath on Flea. 'I should have my Razors chop you into fish food just for having the nerve to show your face!'

'You could have them try,' Flea retorted.

Danny emitted a sudden laugh.

'Ha! You've got some guts, Fletcher, I'll give you that,' he said, glowering again. 'It's just a shame all that schooling doesn't seem to have helped you much in the brains department. Maybe if you'd stayed a Razor instead of tricking Lily into running off with you, you wouldn't have ended up talking yourself into an early grave.'

'If I'd stayed a Razor, an early grave is exactly where I would have ended up. And as for Lily—'

'Lily can speak for herself, thank you very much,' Lily cut in. 'Flea didn't trick me into anything, Uncle Danny. I left because I wanted to. Because I wanted a better life. It's what my mum would have wanted for me, too. It's what she would have wanted for both of us.' Ollie was surprised to see Lily take hold of her brother's hand.

Danny gave a plasticky sneer. 'Well, I hope it was worth it. I hope Dodge thinks it was worth it.' He drew a finger across his face, mimicking the line of Dodge's scar. 'If you ever want to get that seen to, Dodge, I can recommend a good plastic surgeon.'

'No thanks,' Dodge answered. 'I've seen his other work and to be honest I'm not all that impressed.'

Ollie smiled then. He couldn't help it. Danny's gaze fell on him like a spotlight.

'And who's this? A new recruit? You're scraping the barrel a bit, aren't you, Dodge? It's not like you to involve them when they're still wearing nappies.'

'I'm not—' Ollie started to say, but Dodge laid a hand on his arm.

'Ollie's a friend. He's not from the Haven. He shouldn't even be here. He was just about to leave when your toy soldiers out there surrounded us.'

Zeke sniggered. 'You didn't exactly make it difficult for us,' he said. 'I thought you lot were supposed to be good.'

Flea visibly tensed. He shot Ollie a look of pure fury.

'Enough,' said Danny. 'I'm not interested in how you got here, nor in which of you is supposed to be where. All I want to know is what you little sewer rats have done with my Razor.'

'Wait . . . what?' said Erik.

'My missing Razor. The boy you stole. I want him back. *Now.*'

'We don't *steal* kids,' said Erik, sounding only moderately less scared than he looked. 'We set them free, save them from the likes of you.'

Danny's hand had stopped rattling. Instead his knuckles bulged white, as he attempted to crush the dice in his grip.

'You better put a muzzle on your little pet there, Dodge. He barks at me like that again, I'm gonna have to have him put down.'

'Erik's free to say what he likes,' answered Dodge. 'Particularly when he's telling you the truth.'

Ollie didn't like the way this was going. The history between the Haven and Danny's Razors was clearly a lot more fraught than he had realised.

'Do you seriously think we'd have walked into your territory if it was us who'd nabbed your Razor?' Lily was saying. 'There are other kids who've been going missing, too, you know. Other gang members, from all over the city. The cops haven't done anything about it, so we decided we would. *That's* why we came here. To try to find out what's been happening to these kids.'

'Besides,' Flea chipped in, 'what's one missing Razor to you, Danny? Kids like Zeke over there – like me and Lily – we're disposable, aren't we? Isn't that why you use children to do your dirty work in the first place?'

Ollie noticed Zeke shifting uncomfortably. He looked younger all of a sudden, and he glanced towards Danny as though for reassurance. The boss of the Razors didn't even acknowledge that Zeke was there.

'He wasn't just a Razor,' Danny spat. 'The boy who went missing? He's my son. OK? My boy, Harvey. And you took him, just like you took my niece!'

The Haven kids, even Lily and Flea, were taken aback.

'Your *son*?' Dodge repeated.

'Please,' Danny said, 'drop the act. You knew who he was when you stole him from me. Just like you should have known there would be consequences. Now, tell me where he is, or you'll find out how severe those consequences are going to be.'

'It wasn't us!' Sol blurted. 'Maybe you're right, maybe someone took your son for a reason, but do you seriously think we'd be that stupid?'

'You showed up here, didn't you? If that isn't proof of your stupidity, I don't know what is.' Danny gestured to the men in suits. 'Line them up,' he said. 'Against the wall.'

'Hey!' This from Lily, who'd been grabbed first. More Razors had appeared from out of nowhere, and though Ollie and the others tried to struggle, they soon found themselves lined up side by side, each of them held in place by two Razors standing behind them.

Danny held up a single die, pinching it between his thumb and forefinger so that all the Haven kids could see.

'Six numbers, six little sewer rats. You –' he gestured to Ollie, who was at one end of the line – 'are number one. And you –' he sneered at Flea, who was at the other end – 'you're number six. One number each, and whoever's number I roll, that's who I kill first. And then we keep going, until one of you tells me where my son is.'

'Please, Uncle,' said Lily, 'don't do this!'

Ollie looked from her to Dodge, knowing Dodge would say something, do something, to get them out of this, but Dodge looked as helpless as Ollie felt.

'No offence, Fletcher,' said Danny. 'But I sincerely hope my first roll is a six. It's always been my lucky number, you know.' He smiled and rattled his hand, then lowered it to spill the die on to the table.

'Wait!'

Ollie felt all eyes in the room turn towards him. Danny's hand froze centimetres from the baize.

'One roll,' Ollie stuttered. 'Give us . . . one roll.'

'What are you talking about?' Danny's eyes narrowed as they focused on Ollie.

'Look, I . . . I don't know you,' Ollie went on. 'I don't even know these kids I'm with, not really. I only met them a few hours ago.' Was it really so recently that Dodge had burst into

Ollie's life? 'But the thing is,' Ollie said, 'I know they're telling the truth. They *didn't* take your son. I was with them when they found out it had happened. And they came *here*. Lily, Flea, all of them, even though they must have known how you'd respond.'

It was hard to gauge Danny's reaction through his mask-like features, but at the very least he appeared to be mulling over what Ollie was saying.

'So one roll,' Ollie pressed. 'Give us one roll. Whatever number it is, that's how many days we have to find your son and bring him back to you.'

Ollie sensed the others reacting beside him.

'*Us*,' said Danny Hunter. '*We*. I thought you said you didn't know these kids.'

He was right. Without even thinking about it, Ollie had picked a side and cast in his lot with Dodge and the others.

'I don't know them. But I trust them. Just like you should. Killing us isn't going to bring your son back. But if you give us a chance . . . a roll of the dice . . . you won't regret it, I promise you. What have you got to lose?'

For an eternity, it felt like, Danny Hunter didn't respond. He stared, and toyed with the dice in his hand.

'Bring him here,' he said at last.

Ollie found himself being shoved towards the table. Up close, Danny looked even more artificial than he had from half a dozen steps away. It was all Ollie could do not to wrinkle his nose, which was more than Danny Hunter could have managed.

'One roll,' Danny said, holding up one of his burnished yellow dice. He seized Ollie's arm and pressed the die into Ollie's palm. 'I suggest you make it count.'

The die in Ollie's hand felt astonishingly heavy, whether because of the metal or the weight of the responsibility, he couldn't tell. He glanced behind him. Dodge was staring back at him anxiously. Lily nodded at him, once.

Ollie turned to the table. He shook the die the way Danny Hunter had, and dropped it on to the surface. It tipped, tumbled and finally came to a rest.

Ollie looked at what he'd rolled and groaned.

Danny picked up the die. 'You'd better work fast,' he said, smiling. 'Twenty-four hours, my friends. That's how long your new pal has won you. Meaning you have until precisely midday tomorrow.'

There was a murmur of despair among the others. Ollie couldn't look at them as the Razors at his elbows dragged him back to his position in the line.

'With such a small window, I reckon you could use some encouragement,' said Danny, and he held up the die. 'Same rules as before. This time I'm rolling to see which of you gets to stay here as my . . . guest, let's say.'

'Hey!' said Dodge. 'That's not fair!'

'My table,' Danny answered, 'my rules.'

'But if we've only got a day to solve this thing, we're going to need everyone! This is our best team. You can't break us up!'

'I can and I will. Besides, whoever stays, I'll treat them right. For the next twenty-three hours and fifty-eight minutes, anyway. After that, if the rest of you fail to show up with my son . . . Well. I don't need to tell you what will happen after that.'

Danny Hunter grinned, and his cruel grey eyes flashed like one of his crew's razors. He blew into his hand . . . and let the die fall on to the table.

9 ABSENT FRIENDS

The five of them stood shaken on the pavement. They formed a loose, jittery circle, and now they'd been thrown from Danny Hunter's casino, Ollie had no option but to face his friends.

Friends, he thought. That was how he'd been beginning to think of them all, but now he wasn't sure he had that right.

There was Dodge, across from him, looking as shell-shocked as Ollie felt, and who so far hadn't met Ollie's eyes. There was Flea, who by contrast hadn't stopped glaring at Ollie since they'd emerged. Sol, next to Flea, was staring vacantly and silently shaking his head. Beside him was an empty space, as though for their missing member, taken captive by Danny and his ghouls. And then, finally, there was Lily. She was looking at Ollie, though Ollie didn't have the guts to look back at her.

He turned his gaze to the floor. He tried to speak, to tell the others how sorry he was. It was his fault what had happened to Erik, and it was because of Ollie that the rest of them were facing such an impossible task. *One day.* That was all they had to find one missing kid in a city with a population of more than eight million, assuming Harvey Hunter was still in the city at all. And all because Ollie had opened his big mouth.

A hand fell on his shoulder, making Ollie jump. Without Ollie noticing, Dodge had closed the gap between them.

Ollie looked up, and readied himself for whatever was coming. His insides felt as if he'd swallowed cold snails.

But Dodge simply said, 'Well done,' and he smiled.

Ollie, at first, could only blink. 'But . . .' he managed to say, and that was all.

Flea voiced Ollie's astonishment for him. 'You're congratulating him?' he spluttered. 'For what? He just got Erik taken hostage! He got the rest of us lumbered with a task there's not a monkey's chance on Mars we'll be able to accomplish in time! And you're saying *well done*?'

Dodge rounded on Flea. 'Too right I am. If it hadn't been for Ollie, at least one of us would have ended up killed. Maybe you, Flea, in which case Ollie just saved your life.'

'Pah. Danny Hunter was bluffing. He wanted to scare us, that's all. To check we really didn't know where his son was.'

'He didn't look as if he was bluffing to me,' said Sol, moving to Ollie's side.

'That's because he wasn't,' agreed Lily. 'I know my uncle better than anyone, and he doesn't bluff. Not in gambling, not in life. Ollie got us out of there, end of story.'

Flea was casting around, incredulous. 'Seriously?' he said. 'Can none of you see what a liability he is? If it wasn't for him we would never have been ambushed in the first place. And he rolled a *one*, for pity's sake!'

'He bought us twenty-four hours, which is a day more than the rest of us were able to salvage,' said Dodge. 'And finding Harvey Hunter was part of our mission anyway, even if we didn't know it was Danny's son we were looking for. As for the deadline, we were always up against a ticking clock. The only thing that's changed is that suddenly there's a lot more at stake.'

There was a silence, as the remaining Haven members focused their thoughts on their stolen comrade.

'Do you think he'll hurt him?' Ollie asked. 'Danny Hunter. Will he hurt Erik?'

'He'll kill him,' Lily answered, 'no question. But not until our time is up. Until then Danny will stick to his word and keep Erik safe. If it'd been Flea he'd kept hostage, I'm not sure I'd be able to say the same thing.' Lily looked at her brother meaningfully, a warning for him to stop venting his anger on Ollie.

Flea huffed, but said nothing more.

'Is he really your uncle?' Ollie asked Lily. 'Yours and Flea's? What happened to your . . . I mean . . .'

'Our parents?'

Ollie nodded.

'They died when we were kids. Our mum did, anyway. She got cancer. We never knew our father. He left before we were born.'

'He ran off, you mean?'

'Yep. Good riddance, I say. You know, if he didn't have the guts to stick around and look after us. But then, after our mum died, Danny Hunter was our closest living relative. He took us in, and was kind at first. At least to me. Him and Flea, they never really got along.'

'Because I saw him for what he was, that's why,' Flea said, swiping his foot across a patch of pavement.

'He's not all bad,' Lily said. And then, when the others turned to her in surprise, 'Not always, anyway. More bad than good, sure, and in the end that was the reason me and Flea left.'

'I found them on the streets,' Dodge told Ollie. 'They took a bit of persuading, but in the end they joined our cause.'

'At first we figured the Haven was just another gang,' said Lily, 'and we'd had enough of gangs by then to last a lifetime. But then Dodge showed us what the Haven really was. What it stood for. And since then we've never looked back.'

'And that scar,' said Ollie, tentatively tipping his head towards Dodge. 'Danny Hunter gave you that? As, what? Punishment?'

Dodge fingered the line of scar tissue that crossed his face. 'As punishment, yes. But as a warning, too, for us to stay away from his property. Because that's basically how he views his Razors. Not as people, but as things.'

Ollie found himself frowning. In spite of the danger they had known they'd be walking into, Dodge, Flea and Lily – Sol and Erik, too – had gone willingly into Danny Hunter's lair, for the sake of other kids they didn't even know. It was the kind of selfless heroism you only ever read about in comic books.

For a moment the Haven kids appeared taller, unless maybe it was Ollie who felt shorter.

'What about your parents, Ollie?' Lily asked. 'What happened to them?'

Ollie shifted. He didn't like to talk about his parents to anyone, not even to Nancy when she'd been alive. But somehow, with Lily and the others, it felt OK. 'There was a bomb,' he said. 'On a bus. Like, six years ago.'

'I remember that,' said Sol. 'Near Trafalgar Square, right? A sightseeing bus?'

Ollie nodded.

'And your mum and dad were on board?' Lily asked.

Tears had formed in Ollie's eyes. He wiped them away, hoping none of the others had seen. 'They were just walking by. That's all. Just walking by.'

A cloud wandered across the sun, and there was silence for a moment in its shadow.

'We've all got a sob story, PJ,' said Flea, gruffly. 'Every one of us, everyone you'll meet at the Haven: we've all been through more than any kid should.'

There were nods among the rest of the group.

'Well?' said Dodge, after a moment. 'What about it, Ollie?'

'What about what?'

'*Do* you want to meet anyone else from the Haven? Are you coming back with us, or is this the point we say goodbye?'

Once again Ollie looked around, studying the faces of the other members of the group. Flea wanted him to leave, obviously. Sol, Ollie guessed, wanted him to stay. As for Dodge and Lily, after the confrontation with Danny Hunter, Ollie had assumed that they would have agreed with Flea. But then they'd spoken up in his defence.

And there was what had happened to Erik. Given the role he'd played in getting Erik captured, what choice did Ollie really have?

'I'll come back with you,' he said, and he silently welcomed Lily's smile. 'If you'll agree to let me do something first.'

It didn't take them long to reach Ollie's street. They stayed above ground, but moved warily, mindful of running into more Razors. And not just Danny Hunter's gang. If Ollie was right, the closer they got to his flat, the more likely it was that they would also run headlong into the police.

Sure enough, as they rounded the corner into the residential side street, Ollie saw the police cordon around the building that contained his flat. There were forensic officers moving in and out of the doorway, and one, two, three, *four* police cars parked on the street outside.

'Whoa,' said Sol, as he and the others concealed themselves behind a parked delivery van. 'They didn't waste any time. If the police put that many resources into helping to find these street kids who've gone missing, the case would be cracked in no time.' He caught Ollie's frown. 'Sorry, Ollie. I didn't mean . . . I just meant . . .'

'I know what you meant,' Ollie said. 'And you're right, I guess. It's because Nancy's one of them, I suppose. If a cop goes missing, they drop everything to try to find her.'

'Huh,' grunted Flea. 'One rule for them, another for the likes of us.'

'It's not that,' Ollie countered. 'It's just . . . when you're doing something dangerous, like cops do, you need to know there are people who have got your back. Like Erik. He knows you lot are going to do everything in your power to rescue him, right? So if you know there's someone looking out for you, you feel more confident going about your job. Putting your life on the line, sometimes, if that's what it takes.' Ollie shrugged. 'It's just easier when you know you've got friends,' he finished. 'The same way most things are, I guess.'

Neither Flea nor anyone else responded, and Ollie began to wonder if what he'd said had sounded stupid.

But then, 'You got it, Ollie,' Dodge said. 'That's it exactly.'

Ollie tested a smile, then peered again at the activity outside his former home.

'What are we looking for exactly?' Sol asked, gazing out beside him.

Ollie twitched a shoulder. 'Nothing, I guess. I just wanted to check they know she's missing. That someone's looking for her.'

The others maintained a respectful silence. Ollie felt the rhythm of his heart, echoing around the emptiness inside him.

'You realise they'll be looking for you as well, don't you, Ollie?' said Lily gently. 'You're missing, too, as far as the police are concerned.'

Ollie hadn't thought of that. Did that make him a fugitive? Even if the only thing he'd done wrong was not to show the police that he'd been found?

'Maybe I should let them know I'm all right,' Ollie said. 'And that name you mentioned. Maddy Sikes. Maybe I should tell the police about her, so they'll know where to go to look for Nancy.'

'No.' Dodge raised himself upright. 'If you go to the police now, Ollie, the only thing that will happen is that you'll get taken into care. Social services, children's officers, everything. You don't want that, do you?'

Ollie was pretty sure he didn't.

'And besides,' Dodge went on, 'we need you. With Erik gone, we're a man down, and you've already proved what an asset you can be.'

Flea exhaled loudly, but said nothing.

'You can always go to the police later,' Lily said. 'You know, if that's what you decide you should do.'

'And anyway we can help,' said Sol. 'Can't we, Dodge? Once we've found these missing kids and rescued Erik, we can look into Nancy's murder ourselves. Right?'

Dodge didn't look entirely comfortable with the idea, Ollie could tell. But, 'We can make enquiries,' he said. 'Sure.'

Sol beamed at Ollie, as though that were settled.

Ollie looked uncertainly out at the police again. Yes, he felt responsible for Erik, but he was responsible for Nancy, too. How did you make a decision when doing one thing right also meant doing something else that was wrong?

'Let's get going,' Dodge said. 'The clock is ticking, remember? And when we get home, Ollie, there's someone I think you should meet.'

10 GRAND TOUR

Ollie was alone with Dodge.

When they'd reached the Haven, the others had taken their leave in the central lobby. They were going to check in with Jack and Song, to explain about Erik and to find out if there were any more leads. The clock was ticking, and they needed to come up with a plan to rescue him – and fast.

Sol had grumbled about also having schoolwork to catch up on, which he intended to make a start on while he and the others waited for Dodge to join them. It was one of the rules about living in the Haven, apparently. You did your assignments, on time, or else you got put on a warning. Three strikes, and you were out. It was as straightforward as that. No excuses, no exemptions. Without any adults at the Haven to enforce the rules, part of the investigation team's job was to set a good example.

Before Sol and Lily had dashed off, they'd each taken a moment to wish Ollie luck. 'Whatever happens,' Sol had said, 'tell the truth. She can always spot when you're hiding something.'

Who can? Ollie had wanted to ask. *Who exactly am I on my way to meet?*

But neither Sol nor Lily had given him the opportunity, and now he was left stranded in the crumbling mosaic hallway with just Dodge at his side.

Dodge looked at his watch. He'd set a twenty-four-hour countdown, Ollie knew, after the Razors had thrown them on to the street.

'Come on,' Dodge said to Ollie. 'There's something I need to take care of before we head upstairs. And on the way I can give you a tour.' He glanced at his watch again. 'Although it'll have to be the express version, I'm afraid.'

In contrast to the last time Ollie had been in the Haven, there were other children walking in the halls. It was like the period between lessons at Ollie's school.

There was a notable absence of teachers, but even so the kids were incredibly well behaved. They were loud, sure, but there was no running, no fighting, only talking and laughing. Some of the kids were as young as eight or nine, Ollie guessed. One or two seemed older even than Dodge.

For the first time since he'd arrived, Ollie was getting a sense of how many people claimed the Haven as their home.

'At the last count there were one hundred and twenty-two of us,' Dodge said, as though attuned to Ollie's thoughts. 'There's

86

physically space for another two hundred at least, and I wish we could afford to take more kids in. Heaven knows there's plenty out there who could use our help.'

Ollie recalled the argument between Dodge and Flea about why Ollie should be the exception to the ban on new arrivals. He'd never asked to be taken in, but that didn't make him feel any better about using up a spot that could have gone to someone in greater need.

'The youngest children here are eight years old,' Dodge explained. 'The oldest is sixteen. Everyone has to leave before their seventeenth birthday. There are other places they can go if they need help, but the Haven – it's a place for kids.'

Ollie looked again at the children all around them in the corridor. There was no uniform. The clothes the kids wore were just typical kids' clothes: jeans or leggings, T-shirts and hoodies. They were a little ragged here and there, with socks or bare wrists showing on kids that had grown too big for what they were wearing, but on the whole Ollie had the impression that people wore whatever was comfortable.

He wished his school allowed pupils to do that. At St Jerome's, everyone had to wear a tie and, even worse, a *purple* uniform.

Here, there was only one thing to suggest the kids all belonged to the same place. Every kid Ollie passed had a little H somewhere on their person. Some had actual badges pinned to their breasts, some had stitched one on their sleeves. Others – those in vest tops, for example – had simply sketched it with pen on to their bare skin. It wasn't a regular H, though. The middle line was drawn at a slight angle, longer than it should have been, and the letter sat framed by a triangle.

It was like a secret mark or something, Ollie figured. A small symbol of solidarity. It looked pretty cool, he had to admit. Way better than the stupid coat of arms of St Jerome's, which was supposed to be a dragon and a phoenix, but really looked like a pigeon being eaten by a crocodile.

Ollie hadn't spotted the symbol on any of the members of the investigations team. He guessed if they wore one they kept it concealed. He'd only had a glimpse so far into what Dodge and the others got up to, but already he'd learned that there might be times they needed to operate in secrecy. A big H emblazoned on their clothes would kind of give them away.

Dodge saw Ollie looking.

'The H stands for Hogwarts,' Dodge said. 'We're all Harry Potter fans, you see.'

Ollie wasn't certain at first that he was joking. Dodge kept an admirably straight face before finally showing Ollie his dimples.

'Only kidding,' he said. 'It's for the Haven, obviously. And the triangle . . . Did you know that the triangle is the strongest shape in nature? Any external force is spread evenly across its three sides.'

Ollie recalled Mr Mendelssohn, his science teacher, once explaining something similar, though at the time Ollie hadn't really been paying attention. His mind had been on lunch, probably, or the world he was building in Minecraft, or something else he wasn't supposed to be thinking about, the way it tended to be when Ollie was at school. It wasn't that Ollie didn't like learning. He did. It was just the way things were taught that he sometimes took objection to.

Other kids at Ollie's school felt like that as well, Ollie knew, but at the Haven there wasn't a kid who didn't seem to be wearing a smile. It was different here, clearly, even if Ollie didn't fully understand why.

As they walked, Dodge exchanged greetings with the children they passed. He high fived, fist bumped or simply grinned a cheery hello. And he seemed to know everyone's names, just as everyone knew his. Clearly Dodge was something of a celebrity.

The kids seemed to be drifting into the classrooms now, but as the crowd in the corridor was thinning, a little boy of about nine stepped across their path. Dodge and Ollie stopped walking.

'Um,' said the kid, shuffling his feet.

Dodge glanced at Ollie and smiled. He crouched down so he was level with the boy.

'Hey . . . Leo, isn't it?'

The boy nodded.

'What can I do for you, Leo?'

Leo turned crimson, and seemed to be holding his breath. For a worried moment Ollie thought he might be choking.

But then the boy blurted, 'Can I have your autograph?' and thrust a pen and notepad towards Dodge.

Now Dodge was the one to blush. He looked almost as embarrassed as Leo did. 'Well, I . . .'

'Please, Mr Dodge,' the boy said, and Ollie had to half turn away to cover his smile.

Dodge was suppressing a grin, too. 'Sure,' he said, relenting. 'Here.' He scribbled on a page of Leo's notebook and passed it back to him. 'You better hurry,' he said. 'It looks like lessons are about to start.'

The boy didn't take his eyes from Dodge's signature as he continued in a trance towards his classroom.

'*Mr Dodge?*' Ollie said, chuckling, once Leo was out of earshot.

Dodge laughed. 'Tell anyone he called me that and I'll tell everyone I found *you* running around London in your pyjamas.'

Ollie smiled. 'I'll take the secret to my grave,' he vowed.

They walked on. Dodge swept an arm to indicate the now empty hallway. 'So this, obviously, is the teaching wing. All the lessons take place down here. It's where you'll go to school yourself, if you decide to stay with us long term.'

Already Ollie felt a pang of regret at the thought of leaving, but he knew he would eventually have to.

'I . . . won't be here long,' Ollie said. 'Just until we rescue Erik. And . . . you know. You see whether there's anything you can do to help with Nancy.'

Ollie caught something in Dodge's look that suggested he knew something Ollie didn't.

'Well,' he said, 'anyway. *If* you were to stay, this is where you'd go to lessons. The more traditional ones anyway. The curriculum the investigations team follows is slightly . . . enhanced, let's say. There are some special subjects that only we take.'

Ollie was intrigued in spite of himself. 'What kind of special subjects?'

'You know,' said Dodge offhandedly. 'Medical training, survival techniques, counter-espionage. Oh, and hand-to-hand combat.'

Ollie stopped walking. 'Hand-to-hand combat?'

'Karate, really, with a touch of jiu-jitsu.'

Not for the first time – nor the last, he suspected – Ollie was lost for words.

'That sounds . . . useful,' he eventually managed.

Dodge, in response, just smiled.

'Who teaches all this stuff, though?' Ollie asked. 'You said before that there are no adults here. Right? So who takes the lessons?'

Dodge's smile broadened. 'I was wondering when you were going to get around to asking me that.'

Dodge directed Ollie to a door leading into one of the classrooms. There was no window, so Ollie couldn't see inside. After listening for a moment through the woodwork, Dodge knocked and then opened the door wide.

What Ollie saw in the classroom beyond was a circle of maybe a dozen kids, all seated around a rug that didn't quite cover the wooden floor. There was no teacher, though, and no sign of anyone leading the lesson, until one of the children in the circle stood up.

'Sorry to interrupt,' Dodge said. Needlessly, since no one in the room appeared to mind. On the contrary, there was a fizz of excitement among the children, presumably because Dodge had graced them with his presence.

'Ollie,' Dodge went on, 'this is Trish,' and he indicated the girl who'd risen to her feet. She was around twelve or thirteen, with wavy red hair and startled eyes. 'Trish teaches Russian. Isn't that right, Trish?'

'Not today. Today I'm teaching German. As you well know, Dodge. This is supposed to be Erik's class. Where is he?'

'That's actually why we stopped by,' Dodge answered. 'Erik is . . . busy. He's doing something for the investigations team.

It's . . . inescapable, I'm afraid. But he'll be back to take over again soon. A day or two, maximum.'

'A day or two?' Trish echoed. 'Are you serious?'

'It's not ideal, I know,' Dodge said, apologetically.

'I've got my own work to catch up on, you know,' Trish said. 'And my other lessons to teach.'

The other children were following this mutely, their eyes never leaving Dodge.

'I understand,' Dodge said. 'And I'll try to find you some extra cover, I promise.'

He flashed Trish a grin and Trish blushed. She scowled to try to hide it.

'Thanks, Trish,' Dodge said. 'I appreciate it, I really do.' He waved at the kids, who waved back, and he and Ollie backed into the corridor. Wincing, Dodge shut the door behind them. 'She's gonna hate me for ever,' he said to Ollie under his breath. 'Trish is one of the smartest kids here, which means she's always getting stuck doing extra teaching. It's as if we punish her for knowing too much.'

'So it's the *kids* who teach?' Ollie said. '*All* the lessons?'

Dodge led Ollie away from the classroom, walking quickly now back the way they'd come.

'That's right,' he said. 'Not everyone's fluent in four languages the way Trish is. But everyone has *something* to contribute, even if it's just running through stuff with some of the younger kids that you happened to learn the year before. When kids in year eight, say, help kids in year seven, all that stuff is fresh in their minds. And teaching is also one of the best ways to learn, to cement stuff in your memory that's in danger of floating away.'

'You divide into year groups like that? Year eight, year seven, that sort of thing? All the kids in that German class seemed to be different ages.'

'We stick roughly to year groups for the core subjects, but people basically learn at their level. We keep it flexible. What's important is that people get a chance to learn what they need to.'

They'd reached the central hallway and side by side began heading upstairs.

'We try to get everyone helping each other, too,' Dodge went on. 'That's why the classes sit in circles. So if there's no one with the expertise to teach a certain subject, we use textbooks to try to work things out together. We get by pretty well, for the most part. And it's a way of sidestepping the problem that we can't actually afford desks.' He smiled wryly.

'What about exams? Tests and stuff.'

'Yeah,' said Dodge, 'we don't have those.'

Ollie couldn't help but grin. No exams? That sounded too good to be true.

'Seeing as the Haven doesn't officially exist, we can't exactly let the exam boards know who we are. But kids are free to sit exams when they leave, and invariably they pass them with flying colours. And anyway,' Dodge said, 'our philosophy is that it's what you know that counts. Not what you happen to remember the day you're made to take a test.'

It was, thought Ollie: it was as though someone had designed a school with the kids themselves uppermost in mind. Not teachers, not governors, not politics. *Kids*.

They'd reached the second floor. Ollie expected Dodge to lead them along one of the corridors, which ran like spurs from the central hub as they did on the floors below. Instead he continued up the stairs.

'I thought you said you never came up here?'

'I didn't say never,' Dodge replied. 'What I said was we tend to avoid it. You know . . . if we can help it.' He pointed to the floor they were passing. 'The second floor contains the dorms, by the way. The first floor is kind of miscellaneous. It's where a lot of the dull stuff happens – administration, logistics, all that – but the majority of the exciting stuff, too.'

Ollie might have asked Dodge to explain more, but he was all at once focused again on whoever it was they were on their way to meet.

'Because of . . . this person,' Ollie said. 'Whoever we're seeing? Is that why you avoid coming up here?'

'Well . . .' said Dodge, waggling his head. 'Partly. Maybe. For some of us. But for the most part it's like I said. The third floor is literally falling apart, and nasty accidents are the last thing we need. We have some medical expertise, but we're not exactly St Thomas'.'

As soon as they reached the top floor, Ollie could see exactly what Dodge meant. The walls up here were mostly exposed brick, and every other floorboard seemed to be missing. The bannister around the central hallway was absent of most of its supports, meaning if Ollie stumbled (and there was plenty of debris that might trip him up) he would have nothing but his flapping arms to slow his fall towards that mosaic floor in the hallway below. No in-seat entertainment, no drink from the bar, no time even to buckle up his seat belt. Just a lightning-fast flight and a very messy landing.

Dodge walked confidently around the mezzanine, skilfully avoiding the gaps in the floorboards. Ollie quickly fell behind. He was trying to keep as close to the wall as he could, which wasn't easy given that this was also the side of the walkway where the majority of the floorboards were missing.

'So is this person, like, the boss or something?' Ollie called. He'd assumed Dodge was in charge, but he had a vision of a girl sitting on a makeshift throne, a crown on her head and the room around her crumbling to dust. Like a mad princess or something, like out of a story.

'No one's *in charge* exactly, not in the way you mean. If anything Aunt Fay's more a . . . figurehead.'

'*Aunt* Fay?'

'That's what we call her. Her real name's Felicity. Felicity Fagin.'

Ollie was thinking about the 'Aunt' part. 'So is she a grown-up? I thought you said there weren't any grown-ups.'

Dodge laughed. 'I don't think she'd appreciate being called a "grown-up". Aunt Fay sort of defies categorisation.'

'Why do you call her "Aunt" then? And why is everyone so scared of her?'

Dodge was waiting for Ollie to catch up. He'd paused outside a set of double doors, as grand and solid-looking as the oak staircase. If there was a throne room somewhere in this building, this was exactly the sort of entrance that would lead to it.

'Don't be so nervous, Ollie. There's almost certainly nothing to be afraid of.'

'What do you mean, *almost*?'

Rather than answer, Dodge turned and pushed the doors inwards, seeming to bow as he did so. With an ominous creak, the doors into the throne room spread wide.

11 AUNT FAY

Ollie was dazzled by the light. There'd been no electrics in the corridor outside, and the third floor was comparatively gloomy. But when Dodge had opened the doors it was as though he'd whipped back a curtain.

Once his eyes had adjusted, Ollie surveyed what he saw.

This was no throne room, but somehow, miraculously, a *garden*. They weren't outside, though. Ollie could see the side walls, although not where the room ended. Looking at the ceiling, he understood why it was so light. There was more glass than plasterwork. The skylights were frosted, like the windows he'd seen elsewhere in the building, but somehow the sheen of the glass only seemed to make the room brighter. With the greenery, and the slight mist that floated in the air, the overall effect was almost . . . heavenly.

'She's in there somewhere,' said a voice from behind him, and Ollie turned and saw Dodge disappearing along the corridor.

'Aren't you coming?' Ollie called after him.

'I'm going to catch up with the others, try to work out a plan to rescue Erik. We'll come and find you the moment there are any developments. And besides, Aunt Fay likes to meet newcomers on their own. Go ahead. Just mind you don't pick any of her flowers!'

With that Dodge was gone, leaving Ollie standing by himself.

He peered into the room. There was no sign of anyone anywhere, just rows and rows of different plants. Tall ones, short ones, bushy ones, spindly ones. Ollie saw tomatoes growing and what looked like limes, but might just as well have been lemons.

Everything was laid out the way it would have been in a giant greenhouse, like in a garden centre or something, with the planters aligned in rows and separated by narrow paths. There were no missing floorboards in here. Rather, the floor was solid, and carpeted with what appeared to be real grass.

It was hot like in a greenhouse, too. Ollie dragged the sleeves of his hoodie above his elbows and started to wander along the path. He passed through the dense foliage, silently marvelling at what was growing here. It wasn't just fruit. There were flowers so vivid and so vibrant, Ollie would have sworn the petals had been dyed.

After a while he heard the sound of voices, and he veered from the main path so that he was heading towards them.

He came across children tending to the plants. They were all young – among the youngest Ollie had so far seen. Working on their own or in pairs, they were harvesting the fruit, clipping the leaves or doggedly tilling the soil. One or two looked at Ollie as he drew close to them, but most were so absorbed in what they were doing they barely noticed him pass.

Soon Ollie came to a gravel-floored square, almost like a central courtyard. There was a fountain gently gurgling water, and there, on the opposite side of the little square, was the person the others had been so afraid of.

The old woman had her back to him, and was carefully examining one of her plants. She was lightly caressing each leaf, running her brown, weathered fingers first across its surface and then its underside.

'Don't be shy, Ollie Turner. Whatever the others may have said about me, I can assure you I don't bite.'

The woman still had her back to him, and Ollie couldn't help but wonder how she'd known he was there. He'd approached noiselessly, and he hadn't yet stepped from the grass on to the gravel.

Now he did, but the woman didn't turn.

'Are you . . . Aunt Fay?' Ollie asked. He drew to a halt beside the fountain, feeling the spray from the water dapple his cheek. In the heat and humidity of the garden, it was as cool and refreshing as air conditioning.

The woman chuckled. 'Technically I'm neither. But as that's what people around here have taken to calling me, I suppose I must be.'

Aunt Fay brushed her hands together as she turned. She was dressed modestly, in simple trousers and a tunic. Her spongy black hair was speckled with silver, as though she'd been rained on by a cloud of glitter. She wasn't smiling exactly, but it was almost as though she didn't need to. Her features were moulded by kindness, from her high, round cheeks to the laughter lines flaring whisker-like from her eyes.

The thing Ollie noticed about her above all, however, were her eyes themselves. They looked like faded jewels, like jade that has lost its shine. Aunt Fay was blind, Ollie realised.

She stepped towards him, showing no sign in her confident movements of being unable to see. 'I was about to break for a spot of lunch,' she said. 'Would you care to join me?'

She gestured, showing Ollie the pink of her hand, and Ollie noticed a little garden table and two chairs set to one side of the gravel square. On the table's surface was a spread of food. Ollie saw bread, butter, cheese, cherry tomatoes, lettuce and cucumber cut into slices, as well as a pitcher of ice that was melting into water.

There was a growl, and Ollie realised it was his stomach.

'I'll take that as a yes,' said Aunt Fay, chuckling again, and she made space for Ollie to lead the way.

He settled himself on one of the metal chairs. It took all his willpower not to start stuffing himself, and he waited for Fay to offer him a hunk of bread.

'Take three,' she said with a wink. 'But mind you eat some vegetables as well.'

It was the kind of thing Nancy would have said, and Ollie's hunger morphed into something more like sickness. He fed himself a bite of bread anyway, conscious of not being rude, and when he bit down on the oven-warm crust, his hunger reasserted itself with a vengeance. Ollie wolfed down the bread in four mammoth bites, then chased it down his throat with a tomato. The tomato exploded when he bit into it, drowning his taste buds and making Ollie feel momentarily faint. He wasn't sure he'd ever been this hungry, nor eaten food that had tasted this good.

Aunt Fay replaced the basket of bread in exactly the position she'd taken it from, and again Ollie marvelled at how assuredly she moved. And when he looked at her clouded eyes, he would have sworn she could see him in spite of her blindness.

She held her hands clasped together beneath her chin, not yet eating herself, and Ollie noticed something on the back of her left hand. He paused in his chewing, and swallowed more than fitted comfortably down his throat.

'Is something the matter?' Aunt Fay asked.

'No, I . . . your hand, that's all. Your birthmark.'

'Ah.' Aunt Fay smiled, and held her hand out so Ollie could get a closer look. He almost couldn't believe what he was seeing: a tiny H, its middle line longer than it should have been, and the whole thing framed by a triangle. 'I understand some of the children here have taken to decorating themselves with something similar. To think, I'd always been so ashamed of it when I was your age.'

'You mean . . . you could see? When you were young?'

Immediately Ollie regretted asking the question. It felt impolite to ask about someone's disability before they'd raised the subject themselves. Aunt Fay, though, didn't seem to mind.

'I could. Although I must say, I slightly resent the implication that I am now *old*.'

Ollie didn't know what to say. It was hard to guess Aunt Fay's age, because her dark skin had a healthy shine Ollie had only ever seen before on infants. On the other hand, she could not have been younger than seventy, and was perhaps as old as eighty or ninety.

Ollie was trying to decide how best to apologise, when Aunt Fay smiled to show him she'd been teasing.

'I *am* old, Ollie. There's no escaping the fact, I'm afraid. Really I have no business being here, which is why I tend to hide myself away, leave you youngsters to run things the way you think best.'

Ollie's eyes kept being drawn to the remaining chunks of bread on his plate. Aunt Fay passed him the butter. 'Eat,' she insisted. 'Don't stand on ceremony. This is a place for children, which means you eat when you like and how you like, not when some adult says you can.'

Ollie grinned. He took a thin scraping of butter to spread on his bread, then, taking note of what Aunt Fay had said to him, reached for a slice as thick as his finger. The butter was salted to perfection. It melted like ice cream on the still-warm bread.

'How *did* you end up here?' Ollie asked.

'That's a very long story,' said Aunt Fay. 'One best saved, I think, for another day. The concise version is that I've been here since the beginning.'

'The beginning?'

'Nineteen forty-one, to be exact,' said Aunt Fay. 'The year the Haven was set up.'

1941. Ollie wasn't exactly brilliant at history, but he recognised the significance of the date.

'The war,' he declared. 'The Haven was set up during World War Two?'

'It was set up *because* of the war, you could say. You seem to know your history, Ollie. Have you heard of the Government Evacuation Scheme?'

Ollie, munching, nodded. He hadn't heard of the scheme itself, but he knew what it probably related to. 'All the city kids were sent into the countryside. To keep them safe during the bombing. The Blitz.'

Aunt Fay waggled her head to show that he was partly right. '*Some* children were evacuated,' she corrected. 'Not all. There were many of us who were left behind. The weak, the feeble, the poor. The unlucky. Some who were sent away were sent back again, because no one in the countryside would have them.'

Ollie stopped eating. He hadn't heard about *that*. He'd assumed every kid in London had been sent to safety, to live in some grand country house and have adventures, the way it always seemed to happen in books.

'And the evacuations didn't just affect children,' said Aunt Fay. 'Adults were sent away as well. With so many of the men off fighting, London's population was severely depleted. And not just London's, by the way. It was a similar situation in other cities.'

Slowly Ollie resumed chewing. He was mulling over what London must have been like back then: the empty houses, the absent friends, the constant fear of being rained on by a German bomb.

'I was one of the unlucky ones,' said Aunt Fay. 'Or at least, that's the way it seemed at the time. And then, when my parents were killed in an explosion, I was effectively in London all alone. It was a difficult time,' she concluded sadly, and her unseeing gaze seemed to turn momentarily inwards.

'So the Haven . . .' Ollie said. 'Someone set it up to take care of all the kids who were left behind?'

Aunt Fay smiled. 'It wasn't quite as straightforward as you make it sound, but yes, that's essentially what happened.'

Again she seemed lost for a moment in her memories, her cheerful features shadowed by regret.

'You,' Ollie said, catching on. '*You* set the Haven up.'

'I played a part,' Aunt Fay conceded. 'A small one. Others, friends of mine, deserve the greater credit. There were others like me, you see. Other children who were abandoned and frightened and alone. With so many teachers evacuated as well, there were no school places for us, and more importantly many of us had lost our homes. So the Haven . . . it became a refuge. An unofficial one, but a refuge nonetheless. A place to sleep and to learn and to draw comfort from the presence of friends.'

She ran a fingertip across the birthmark on her hand, blindly tracing the outline of the H.

'So the Haven's existed all this time?' Ollie asked. 'From 1941 until now?'

'There have been ups and downs, shall we say, but yes, the Haven has been in existence all this time. We assumed when we first established it that the need would only be temporary, perhaps until the end of the war. But as the years have passed, that need has not diminished. The Haven is as important now as it ever was, which is what makes our current circumstances so hard to bear.'

'What do you mean?' Ollie asked.

Aunt Fay forced out a smile. It was the saddest smile Ollie had ever seen.

'What I mean, Ollie, is that the Haven is dying. And I am afraid it may be too late to save it.'

12 DYING LIGHT

Ollie looked down at his plate. Gently, he pushed it away.

'I've put you off your food,' said Aunt Fay. 'I'm sorry, Ollie.'

'No, that's . . . I'm full. Thank you. That was delicious.'

Aunt Fay seemed to appreciate his politeness. 'Perhaps you'll have some more later. I must say, I've fairly lost my appetite myself.' She stood carefully, and held out her hand. 'Come,' she said. 'Walk with me. Let's enjoy this wonderful garden while we still can.'

Ollie hesitated, then took Aunt Fay's hand as he rose. Her skin felt cool, and soft like supple leather.

'You'll have to help me, if you don't object,' she said, threading her arm through his. 'I know this garden like I know my own soul, but that doesn't mean I'm immune to the occasional misstep.'

They began to walk, and though Ollie was in theory the one guiding, it was Aunt Fay who determined the direction. They headed deeper into the garden, down a path Ollie hadn't yet taken.

'What you said just now,' Ollie ventured, 'about the Haven dying. Did you mean . . . the building or . . .' He was thinking of the missing floorboards, the plaster crumbling from the walls.

Aunt Fay shut her eyelids and inhaled deeply before she answered. They were passing through a tunnel of flowers, and the perfume in the air was so thick Ollie felt almost as though he might have scooped it in his palms. It smelt like Nancy, like her neck when she hugged him.

Aunt Fay exhaled with a sigh. 'The building is part of it, of course,' she said. 'It's a bit like me, I'm afraid. Willing, in principle, but weak in flesh.'

'But it could be repaired. Couldn't it?'

Aunt Fay tipped her head from side to side: not a no, not a yes. 'It would take a lot of money. A *lot* of money. Money, I'm afraid, we don't have.' She laughed suddenly. 'I say *we*. I keep forgetting it is no longer my responsibility. The future of the Haven is in others' hands. Lily's, Song's, Fletcher's, Erik's, Soloman's, Jacqueline's. All the other children, too. They are the ones who carry the burden now.'

Ollie felt a pang at the mention of Erik. He wondered if Aunt Fay knew what had happened to him; how the others were working on a plan to save him even as they spoke. From the way she'd voiced his name so casually, he suspected she didn't.

'And Dodge,' Ollie said. 'You didn't mention Dodge.'

'And Dodge, of course,' agreed Aunt Fay. 'Dodge more than anyone recognises the weight of his responsibility. In fact I can't help worrying that he has taken on too much. He makes many of the hard decisions by himself, when the burden would surely feel lighter if it were shared.'

Ollie pondered for a moment. 'Dodge knows what he's doing,' he said at last. 'I'm sure of it.'

Aunt Fay turned and smiled, her arm still hooked around Ollie's elbow.

'I hope so, Ollie. But closing the Haven's doors, for example, as Dodge has done. Banning new arrivals . . .' She shook her head. 'Again, as I say, it is not my decision, and I understand that resources are stretched. Yet the Haven's strength has always been in its openness, its willingness to take people in. It's in diversity that we thrive.'

'But if you can't *afford* to help anyone else, what other option does the Haven have?'

Aunt Fay smiled wryly. 'That, indeed, is the question. But there is a short-term view and a long-term one. Much of our income, over the years, has come from donations from the people we have helped. So a child comes here when they are young. We shelter them, educate them, help them find a job, and then, once they are earning, they are generous enough to send us something from their salary, to help us help *other* children. It is like a lifecycle,' Aunt Fay said, as she trailed her fingers through the foliage of the plants that they passed. 'One thing supports the other.'

'So what's changed?'

'What's changed is, the fewer children we help, the fewer adults there are later to help *us*. That is the consequence of Dodge's policy that I am afraid he does not quite see.'

Ollie wasn't sure what to say to that.

'Did you know,' said Aunt Fay, 'that at its peak the Haven gave shelter to over three hundred children? Now we are merely a fraction of that.'

'Isn't there . . .? I don't know. Someone who could help? The government, say. The Haven is kind of like a charity, after all. It's like a school as well. So couldn't the government give you money and stuff? The way it does for other schools?'

'The government doesn't know we exist. If they did, they would shut us down in an instant.'

'But . . . why?'

'Because as you say, Ollie, the Haven represents charity in its purest form. Which means no regulation, no interference, no *politics*.' She said the last word with distaste. 'The Haven is about children helping children, remember? What adult have you ever met who doesn't believe grown-ups always know best? Present company excluded, I hope.'

She gave a smile, and Ollie showed half a smile back.

'No, Ollie. If the government found out what we were doing here – what Dodge and his team were doing all the more, the danger they so often put themselves in – the Haven would be finished. The government would send the children here to care homes or refugee centres or back to the war zones they fled from.'

'So that's the reason for all the secrecy,' Ollie said. 'The hidden entrance, the frosted glass, the fingerprint scanners . . .'

There was a glitch in Aunt Fay's movements. 'Fingerprint scanners? We have fingerprint scanners?' She grinned like a little girl, and shook her head in wonder. 'My, my.'

Ollie couldn't help but smile, too. 'There's facial recognition as well. Secret cameras hidden in the brickwork. Didn't you know?'

Aunt Fay shook her head again and tittered. 'I did not. I suppose no one thought to tell me because they knew I would never have call to use them. I haven't left this building in . . . Well. I don't care to think about how long.'

She and Ollie ambled on.

'So all this time the Haven has remained a secret?' Ollie said. 'Since 1941?'

Aunt Fay bobbed her head – proudly, Ollie would have said. 'All this time,' she confirmed.

'*How?*' Ollie asked.

Aunt Fay chuckled. She had a nice laugh, Ollie thought. It was exactly like a little kid's.

'First off,' said Aunt Fay, 'and most important, everyone who passes through the Haven's doors understands precisely what is at stake: the number of lives that would be permanently damaged if they betrayed the secret they've been entrusted with. Our pupils take a sacred oath, but I'm not even sure it's necessary. You've been here, how long? Hours, really. You have no loyalty to the Haven, Ollie. And yet, if you were asked to reveal our existence, would you?'

Ollie didn't even have to think. 'I wouldn't. Also, though, I *couldn't*. I have no idea where we are.'

Aunt Fay inclined her head, acknowledging Ollie's point. 'That's another form of protection. Our pupils are free to come and go as they please, but they only ever enter and exit through the tunnels. Very few could look at a map of London and pinpoint the Haven's exact location. Not – again – that they would want to. And besides,' Aunt Fay added, with another chuckle, 'who would believe them if they did?'

'But what about people passing by? On the street or whatever?'

'The Haven, from the outside, is entirely unremarkable. Just another indistinct London building, beautiful in its way but as run-down on the outside as it is within. Most people passing by would assume the building had been abandoned.'

For some reason Ollie thought of Danny Hunter's secret casino, how if it hadn't been for Zeke and the Razors, Ollie and the others would have walked right past it without ever knowing what went on inside. And there were dozens of buildings like that even on Ollie's walk to school: blocks he'd never seen anyone either enter or leave, whose contents he could only have guessed at.

'It's amazing what people don't notice when it's right in front of them,' said Aunt Fay, as though reading Ollie's thoughts.

'What about the government, though? The council. Surely there are, like, records and stuff. At the very least enough to get people asking questions.'

'The government *owns* the Haven,' Aunt Fay told him, with a glint.

'But you said—'

She held up a hand to cut him off. 'The government owns the Haven, but they don't *know* they own it. That's our final layer of protection, Ollie. Our former pupils, when they leave, they don't just keep our secret. They also help us guard it.'

'In what way?'

'In whatever way they can. The Haven's graduates are exceedingly well educated, a tribute to the system we have in place here, as well as to their own enthusiasm to learn.' Aunt Fay adjusted her hold on Ollie's arm. 'The end result is, there are former Haven pupils in all sorts of high-level jobs. We've had an ambassador, a chief executive, even a PM.'

'A prime minister?' exclaimed Ollie, coming to a halt.

'A project manager,' replied Aunt Fay. 'For Google. Far more useful to our needs than a mere politician, I can assure you.'

They resumed walking.

'So these people help to cover our tracks,' Aunt Fay went on. 'The government owns the building we're standing in, but thanks to one of our former pupils, there is no record to say that it does.'

They turned another corner, and Ollie realised they were back where they'd started. Aunt Fay had led him in a circle, so that before them was the fountain and their little table, exactly as they had left it.

Aunt Fay lowered herself on to the concrete surround beside the pool of water. She gestured for Ollie to join her.

'But that is what I meant when I said I feared the Haven was dying,' said Aunt Fay. 'Physically, yes, in that there are already large sections of this building we dare not use. But the Haven is also an *idea*. And ideas wither when there is no one around to believe in them. The fewer children we help, the fewer adults there will be to help us. Our funding has already dried up and I fear the protection we receive will be next.'

Ollie glanced across, and was horrified to see a tear trailing down Aunt Fay's cheek.

'I must apologise,' she said. 'I didn't mean to burden you with an old woman's worries. What about you, Ollie? You have heard our story. What is yours?'

'I . . . I don't really have one.'

Aunt Fay laughed, and the sound to Ollie's ear was like a burst of music.

'Come now,' she said. 'Everyone has a story, just as no one knows how each chapter will unfold, nor how their story will end. Tell me how you came to be here, for example. How it is that I am sitting next to you in this garden.'

Ollie shifted. He never liked to talk about himself, and he had no desire to stir up all the sadness he was feeling about Nancy. But it was like with Lily and the others: with them talking about his life had seemed OK. With Aunt Fay that feeling went further. More than OK, it seemed . . . natural. Almost as though he were talking to Nancy herself.

And so he told her. Not just about Nancy and how Dodge had found him. He told Aunt Fay about his parents dying, too. How he wished he'd been able to save them, the way he should have been able to save Nancy.

'I could have helped her,' he heard himself saying. 'I *should* have helped her.'

By the time he was finished, Ollie was in tears himself. They were the tears he'd been holding back since this had begun. But now he couldn't have stopped them if he'd wanted to.

Aunt Fay wrapped her arm around Ollie's shoulders. She comforted him until he was all cried out.

Ollie pulled back from her eventually, feeling foolish. But there was no denying that he also felt better, as though he'd been carrying something heavy and someone else was now helping him with the burden.

He smiled at Aunt Fay and the old woman mirrored it, as though she'd registered it with some sense that wasn't sight.

'I could tell you that what happened wasn't your fault, Ollie, but it seems to me that you are not quite ready to believe that. But you will,' she said, patting his hand again. 'Given time, and reflection, you will. In the meantime know that you are with friends, and that I for one am delighted to have you here. I was curious to meet you when I found out Dodge had made an exception to his rule, and I can see now exactly why he did.'

Ollie flushed again, partly with shame this time, because Aunt Fay didn't seem to realise that he would soon be leaving.

He was just about to try to tell her when a voice behind Ollie made him turn.

'Ollie?'

Ollie looked and saw Lily at the head of one of the paths, red faced and out of breath.

'Lily?' said Aunt Fay. 'Is that you? Whatever's the matter?'

Lily edged forwards on to the gravel. 'I'm sorry to interrupt, Aunt Fay. But, Ollie?' Lily fixed Ollie with urgent eyes. 'You need to come with me.'

'What is it?' Ollie said. 'Is it something to do with Erik?'

'Maybe,' said Lily. 'I don't know. There was a girl, in the tunnels. She must have followed us, or . . .' She shook her head.

'I don't know how she found us, but she did. So we brought her in and . . .'

Ollie was watching Lily intently, waiting for whatever was coming.

'She says she knows you, Ollie. This girl, this stranger, she says she's here because of you.'

13 LILY HUNTER

It struck Ollie as he trailed after Lily that he'd barely offered Aunt Fay a proper goodbye. He'd been caught up in the moment, infected by Lily's sense of urgency, but as he followed her towards the main staircase, it occurred to him that he might never see Aunt Fay again.

'Jack spotted her on one of the cameras,' Lily said, and Ollie realised she was talking about the stranger, the girl who'd claimed she knew Ollie. He and Lily were hurrying as best they could towards the top of the staircase, dodging the pitfalls and missing floorboards that lined the way. 'She hadn't got as far as finding the entrance to the Haven, but she was searching the tunnel walls, looking for some kind of doorway. So Dodge made the call, told Song to head down and bring her in. We're keeping her in the kit room for the time being, until we figure out who she is.'

'She didn't tell you?' Ollie asked.

'She wouldn't tell us anything,' Lily replied. 'Said she would only talk to you. She didn't mention you by name, but she described you. Your hair, your height, everything –' Lily winced apologetically – 'right down to the dinosaurs on your pyjamas.'

Ollie might have flushed at this, but for the time being he was too confused.

He and Lily reached the top of the staircase. As they started down, Lily touched him lightly on the elbow. Ollie jerked in surprise.

'It's OK, you know,' Lily told him.

Ollie's fingers grazed the place where Lily had touched him. 'What do you mean?'

'Just . . . you know. Getting upset. Practically everyone does when they talk to Aunt Fay. She kind of has that effect on people. That's why some of the kids here – some of the boys, in particular – are so reluctant to go and see her.'

It hadn't occurred to Ollie until now, but Lily couldn't have failed to notice the redness of his eyes. And when she'd interrupted them in the garden, Ollie had only just managed to control his tears.

This time Ollie did flush. He couldn't stop himself.

'Sorry, I didn't mean to embarrass you,' Lily said.

'No, that's . . . It's fine.' Ollie tried to hide his face without *looking* as if that was what he was doing.

'You should have seen the state of me after I first met her,' Lily went on. 'And Flea. If anything Flea was even worse, sobbing on my shoulder like a baby.' She caught Ollie's eye and gave a grin. In spite of his embarrassment, Ollie couldn't help but return it.

'He's not the idiot he pretends to be, you know,' Lily said, as she and Ollie continued down the stairs. 'My brother, I mean. He's just . . . frustrated, I guess.'

'Frustrated?'

Lily waggled her head, as though it wasn't quite the word she'd been reaching for. 'It's like, he believes in the Haven more passionately than anyone I know. As much as Aunt Fay, almost. And he sees Dodge's point, about not being able to take more people in. On the other hand, he doesn't like it. If it were up to Flea we'd be trying to help *everyone*.'

Ollie was too startled to respond. He'd had Flea pegged as a survival-of-the-fittest-type guy, someone who believed in helping himself first, others later.

'He's grateful, too, you know,' Lily said. 'Even if he's too pig-headed to show it.'

'Grateful? For what?'

They'd reached the first floor, and started down the final flight of stairs side by side.

'For you saving him. From Danny Hunter. And, well . . . I'm grateful, too.'

Before Ollie knew what was happening, Lily leant across and kissed him on the cheek. Ollie wobbled where he stood. He was glad they were near the bottom of the staircase, because for a second he worried he might fall.

Lily continued on. 'We should hurry,' she said. 'The others will be waiting.'

'Right,' Ollie said, discombobulated.

'And . . . Ollie?' Lily stopped and turned to face him. She wasn't as red as Ollie felt, but there was a definite glow to her cheeks. 'Don't tell Dodge I did that, will you?'

'Dodge? No, I . . . Of course not. But . . . why would Dodge care?'

Lily looked down and shuffled her feet. 'Me and Dodge, we're kind of together.'

Ollie felt the warmth in his cheeks turn into a burn. 'Together? You mean . . .'

'He's my boyfriend. We don't go around shouting about it. We don't want it interfering in investigations. He's not the jealous type, but I wouldn't want him – or anyone – to get the wrong idea.'

There was a pointedness to Lily's words that Ollie couldn't have missed if he'd wanted to. The fizz in his stomach went flat.

Dodge and Lily. Lily and Dodge. Ollie must have been blind. Of *course* Lily would fancy Dodge. Of course Dodge would fancy Lily.

'No,' Ollie said. 'Right. Of course.'

Lily twitched a smile and walked on, across the mosaic floor. For a second Ollie stood and watched her go. He felt numb, mainly, but also oddly relieved. Maybe leaving the Haven wouldn't be quite as difficult as he had thought.

14 STREET LEVEL

When they reached the kit room, the entire team – minus Erik – was there.

Sol, Jack and Dodge were conferring in a corner. Flea and Song were facing the lockers, forming a human wall, and it took Ollie a moment to realise they were standing guard.

The stranger – the prisoner – was seated on one of the benches, and Flea was looming menacingly over her. Song stood with her feet slightly apart, her body angled to make herself narrow. Ollie remembered what Dodge had said, that the investigations team all took karate lessons. Everything Ollie knew about self-defence was limited to the fairly basic moves Nancy had taught him, but it was obvious even to him that Song, the mathematics whizz, knew how to handle herself.

After one look at the girl they'd taken captive, Ollie was certain he didn't recognise her. She was about his age, Ollie guessed, with dark skin and hair, and a thin, boyish frame. She was covered in grime, the way Ollie had been when he'd emerged from the sewers. Her hands in particular were black. Ollie imagined her feeling her way along the walls of the tunnel, hunting for the entranceway she never quite found.

Which made Ollie wonder: if she didn't know where the entranceway was, what had made her so certain it was there?

'That's him,' the girl said, her accusing finger spearing the space between Flea and Song. Her defiant eyes had fixed on Ollie.

Ollie found himself shrinking, feeling guilty for something he didn't know he'd done.

'Ollie?' said Dodge. 'Do you know this girl?'

Flea and Song parted to offer Ollie a better view, and he looked again at the girl seated on the bench. She was glaring at him, almost daring him to deny it.

Ollie started to shake his head. 'I—'

'I didn't say he knew *me*,' the girl interrupted. 'What I said was I knew *him*. He was there. In the building. Where that mad cow had us locked in the basement.'

And then, suddenly, Ollie remembered: running from the men who'd killed Nancy, shutting himself behind the door . . . and seeing a pair of eyes staring up at him through the dark. Gollum eyes, he'd thought at the time, but looking at the girl in front of him, he realised the eyes he'd seen had been hers. They shone out from her dirt-smeared face as intently as they had through the darkness.

'He dropped this,' the girl said, dangling a key. 'Not that I needed it in the end. You left the door hanging from its hinges. I followed you out and down into the sewer.'

Dodge and Ollie exchanged a glance, as they silently shared the memory of their escape.

'I could see he wasn't alone,' the girl continued, 'but I didn't get a proper look at whoever was helping him. One of you lot, I'd bet.' She fixed her eyes on Dodge, having noticed the way he'd looked at Ollie. 'Nice move, by the way: using the sewer to escape. The only thing I couldn't figure out was how I lost you in the tunnels. One moment you were there and then you were gone. I guessed there must have been a hidden door or something. Turns out I was right.'

She flicked her eyes towards the ceiling, surveying the space around her.

'You're that Haven lot,' the girl declared, 'aren't you? Is that where we are? At the Haven? I have to say, from all the stories I've heard, I was expecting something a bit more impressive.'

'This is just the—' Sol started to say, until Jack elbowed him in the ribs.

The stranger looked at Sol and smirked. 'I always thought the Haven was a myth. Now I see it's basically a dump. And you lot . . . the rumours were you could come and go like ghosts. Turns out you're just a bunch of losers, paddling through sewage in the dark.'

Ollie noticed Flea curl his fingers into fists, but it was Lily who stepped forwards to speak. 'Did no one teach you that guests were supposed to be polite?' she said. 'Talk like that is liable to get you thrown out.'

The girl rose to her feet. Standing she was shorter than Song, but she appeared equally as tough, and just as ready for a fight. 'I'm not going anywhere,' she stated. 'Not until blondie over there tells me what the hell is going on. Why the hell I was taken captive!'

Ollie blinked. It was Dodge who gave voice to his surprise.

'Why should Ollie know any more than you do?'

'Ollie, is it?' the girl mocked. 'I used to have a gerbil named Ollie. He even looked like you,' she went on. 'Same fuzzy hair, same chubby cheeks. And about as handy in a fight, I expect.'

Ollie reddened. Not so much because of what the girl had said. More at Flea's surreptitious sneer.

Lily took another step forwards. 'Didn't I warn you to be more polite?'

'Look,' put in Jack, and she manoeuvred her wheelchair into the centre of the room. 'Insulting each other isn't going to get us anywhere. How about we make some proper introductions, and then we start answering one another's questions?'

Jack turned her stare on Lily, then back to the stranger. It was a teacher's stare, Ollie would have said, and briefly he found himself hoping he wouldn't ever have to take one of Jack's classes.

'Fine,' said Lily, turning away. The stranger scowled, and sulkily dropped back on to the bench.

Her name was Keya, it turned out, and she ran with a gang Ollie hadn't heard mentioned yet. The Forzas, named after an Xbox game, one Ollie had played himself. Not her choice, Keya insisted, but her stupid brother's. He was in charge of the Forzas, a group of maybe thirty kids who ran one of the roughest estates in Brixton. Keya was his second in command.

'And I can guarantee he's tearing the place apart looking for me,' Keya told them. 'He'll blame the Southsiders, probably. They're our rivals, from the estate next door. Another bunch of losers, if you ask me.'

'So why didn't you head straight back home?' Song asked her, ignoring the pointed comment. 'Why bother following Ollie and Dodge through the tunnels if you knew your brother was so desperate to find you?'

Keya looked at Song like she was stupid. 'It was a way out, wasn't it? And I'm not gonna go home without finding out who took me, am I? My brother would throw me right back out on to the street again.'

Some brother, Ollie thought.

'So who did take you?' This from Sol, even though Ollie had a feeling Sol already knew the answer. They all did. Ollie could tell from the way Dodge, Flea and the rest of the investigations team were looking at each other.

Maddy Sikes. The person who'd kidnapped Ollie, and who was responsible for Nancy's murder.

Ollie must have said the name aloud without realising it, because all of a sudden everyone in the room was looking at him, Keya included.

'Maddy Sikes?' she said. 'Is that the crazy woman? The woman who had us thrown in the basement? Cropped white hair, blinging jewellery, smile like she wants to eat you alive?'

'That's her all right,' Sol confirmed.

'I *told* you,' said Flea, ignoring the rest of them and confronting Dodge. 'I said to you that's where the missing kids are.'

'But . . . there was no sign,' said Dodge. 'I searched the warehouse. I *did*.'

'You must have missed something,' said Flea, angrily. 'But PJ here must have seen them. If Keya saw *him*. Right?' He rounded on Ollie. 'Well, PJ? What have you got to say for yourself?'

This time the guilt Ollie felt was entirely real. He *had* seen Keya, just like Flea said. 'I-I saw a pair of eyes,' he stuttered. 'That's all. And I . . . I didn't know anyone was missing. Not at the time. I was thinking about . . . about Nancy. And . . . trying to get away. And . . .' He trailed off, conscious how flimsy his explanation must have sounded.

Flea huffed and spun away, as though Ollie had just proved everything Flea had been saying about him all along.

'It's not Ollie's fault,' said Sol. 'How can it be?'

'Of course it isn't Ollie's fault,' Jack agreed, turning her teacher's glare on Flea. 'And anyway, none of that matters. What matters is what we do now.'

'You said "us",' said Dodge, talking to Keya. 'How many other kids were in that basement?'

Keya shrugged. 'Twenty? Thirty maybe? They were all from other gangs, so I kept myself to myself. That's how come I escaped but they didn't. They were all huddled at the other end of the basement, probably didn't even see me slip out.'

Flea turned to face the others.

'So now we know for certain,' he said. 'Maddy Sikes is the one who's been kidnapping the kids, which means she's got Harvey Hunter, too. And if we rescue Harvey Hunter, we rescue Erik. Right?' He glanced around, but didn't wait for anyone to answer. 'So what are we doing standing around looking pretty? Let's get going, back to the warehouse.' He marched towards the door.

'Wait,' said Dodge. 'We can't be sure. Not yet. We shouldn't just assume—'

'Of course we should!' insisted Flea, cutting him off. He turned to Keya. 'Harvey Hunter,' he said. 'Danny Hunter's son. Was he there? In the basement with you?'

'How should I know?' said Keya. 'I'm not blooming Facebook, am I?'

'What do you think, Dodge?' said Jack. 'I never thought I'd say this, but I reckon Flea's right. Harvey Hunter has to be there. They *all* must.'

'But why on earth would Maddy Sikes kidnap kids?' said Sol. 'Isn't she into, like, financial fraud? Smuggling, stolen art, things like that. High-level stuff. She *never* gets involved with gangs. Reckons all that street-level stuff is beneath her.'

'Maddy Sikes is into anything that makes her money,' answered Jack. 'Money or power, although in her mind they're basically the same thing.'

'Yeah, but even so,' said Sol. 'How's she gonna make any money out of kidnapping kids?'

'Ransoms, maybe?' put in Song.

Keya gave a snort. 'Like my brother would ever pay a ransom for me. Like he could *afford* to.'

'Keya's right,' said Dodge. 'And think about it: all the kids who've gone missing are from the streets. Which means *no one's* going to pay a ransom for *any* of them. Certainly nothing big enough to interest Maddy Sikes.'

'So . . . what then?' said Sol. 'What's in it for her?'

There was the sound of thinking, broken only when Ollie cleared his throat.

'You said they were gang members,' he said. 'Right? Like, from rival gangs? All the kids who've gone missing?'

'Leave this to the grown-ups, PJ,' said Flea, derisively. 'You've done enough damage already, don't you think?'

'Flea!' protested Lily.

'Yeah, Flea – button it,' said Sol.

Flea glowered, but stayed silent when he saw how the others were looking at him.

'Go on, Ollie,' said Dodge, encouragingly. 'Finish what you were going to say.'

'Keya said her brother would blame their main rivals,' Ollie said. 'The gang next door. The . . . what did you call them?'

'The Southsiders,' said Keya. 'Knowing my brother, he's probably already started trying to get payback.'

'How do you mean?' asked Jack.

'Like, picking fights, invading their territory. If a rival gang nabs one of your members, you can't just take it lying down.'

Ollie nodded. 'That's kind of what I was thinking.' He looked across and saw Dodge frowning. 'Keya's the second in command of her gang. Harvey Hunter is Danny Hunter's son. I don't know for sure, but I'd bet all the other kids who've gone missing are high up in their gangs, too. Or, if not high up, then important somehow. Like, someone's son, someone's sister . . .'

He looked at Jack, who nodded, confirming his point.

'So,' Ollie continued, 'if the kids aren't being taken for ransoms, they must have been kidnapped for some other reason.'

'Well, *duh*,' said Flea, but Lily shushed him. Her look told Ollie to go on.

'Maddy Sikes isn't trying to make money,' he said. 'Not immediately, anyway. Probably this is part of some bigger scheme: the first stage in some grand master plan. What she's trying to do is get the gangs fighting one another. *All* the gangs, right across the city.' He checked to see if anyone was following him. 'Don't you see? Maddy Sikes is looking to start a war.'

15 PHASE TWO

Maddy Sikes stood regarding the mended door. She was thinking of horses, of that saying about shutting the stable door after the horse has already bolted.

'Just one, you say?' she said to Grimwig, who was silently awaiting her pronouncement on the matter of who should be punished.

'Just one. The Brixton girl. The one with the mouth.'

Sikes knew exactly who Grimwig was referring to. As Sikes's underlings had dragged the girl – Freya, was it? Keya? – into the basement, she'd hurled a torrent of expletives across her shoulder, words a girl of her age had no business knowing.

Sikes had watched on with interest. She liked it when her prey put up a fight. It made the kill, when it came, all the sweeter. Also, the girl reminded Sikes of one of the bullies who had made her life such a misery at the boarding school she'd been forced to attend. Alice Crookshank, a foul-mouthed, vicious creature, who Sikes had eventually claimed as the first of her ninety-nine victims. It had been an act of revenge so sweet, it had almost made the years of bullying worthwhile.

Almost.

But the girl. Unlike Alice Crookshank, she'd got away. Escaped, the same way Ollie Turner had, presumably. And all because of him, too. If he hadn't run. If he hadn't gone poking his nose behind doors he had no right to open . . .

'Why wasn't I informed about this earlier?' Sikes asked Grimwig.

'No one thought to do a headcount until a couple of hours ago.'

Sikes pursed her immaculately painted lips. 'And which idiot left the key in the lock in the first place?'

Grimwig moved only his eyes, indicating the two guards standing nervously against the opposite wall.

Sikes turned, and Bullseye, who had so far been waiting obediently at her heel, took this as a signal. The dog edged towards the two men and gave a growl: a low, ominous rumble from deep behind his needle-sharp teeth.

The younger, slimmer of the two guards stepped forwards. 'We're sorry, Ms Sikes, honest we are. Bulger, he said it would save time and—'

'Time?' said Sikes, cutting him off. 'You call this – my being here – saving time?'

Bullseye growled again and the guard shook his head with a whimper. He cowered back against the wall.

Sikes turned to the older, fatter man. Bulger. How appropriate, Sikes thought, looking at his belly protruding over his belt buckle.

'It was your decision?'

The big man was positively wobbling with fear. When he shook his head, his jowls quivered, too. 'That's a lie,' he claimed. 'Timmons here –' he nodded towards the thin man – 'he's the one who said it would save time. He's always skipping duties. Always late, always trying to clock off early. He's lazy, is what he is. It's his fault the girl got away.'

Sikes looked again at Timmons, who was wide-eyed at Bulger's accusations. Sikes could tell exactly which man was lying.

She made her decision.

'You,' she said to Timmons, 'stand over there. Your punishment is that you get to clean up the mess.'

Timmons's relief was coloured by confusion. He shuffled across to the opposite wall, nervously bypassing Bullseye on the way. 'But . . . what mess, Ms Sikes?' he said, one eye on the enormous husky, the other scanning the bare corridor.

Maddy Sikes didn't reply. She turned away, and Grimwig fell into place at her shoulder. As they marched away along the passageway, Bullseye's growls, behind them, grew louder. There was a scream, more high-pitched than Sikes would have expected from such a big man – and then the scream was abruptly cut off.

They were on the warehouse floor by the time Bullseye caught up with them. His tongue was lapping across his teeth, as though he was trying to remove what looked like lipstick from his snow-white fur.

Sikes reached down and smoothed a hand along his back.

So, one hundred, she said to herself. Bulger hadn't exactly been the memorable figure she'd had in mind for her landmark victim, but his death had been unavoidable, and it made no sense to put it off. Maddy Sikes didn't tolerate mistakes. She tolerated slovenliness and deceit even less.

It had half crossed Sikes's mind to blame Grimwig himself for what had happened. He was the one who'd hired Bulger, after all, which made him indirectly responsible for the man's mistakes.

Sikes would have to keep an eye on her assistant, as well as looking out for potential replacements. There was one person who might do, Sikes thought. Yes indeed; there was one person who might do very nicely. They would have to be trained, and properly motivated, and Sikes would have to see how they performed in the audition they didn't know they were currently taking. But maybe, soon . . .

Sikes returned her attentions to the matter in hand.

In front of her, in the warehouse, a vast clear-up operation was underway. The shipment had already been moved on, ready to be deployed into position, and a battalion of men in white over-suits were meticulously going about their tasks. It was crucial that no traces were left behind, no potential evidence overlooked. With Nancy Bedwin out of the picture, chances are no one would come looking, but Sikes couldn't permit any more errors. One escaped prisoner she could tolerate – if having the man responsible ripped to shreds by her attack dog counted as being tolerant – but with this aspect of her plan, the stakes were higher. One little oversight here, and everything Sikes had been preparing for would come undone.

'How much longer?' Sikes asked Grimwig.

'Another hour. Two, maximum.'

Ahead of schedule. Sikes bobbed her head appreciatively.

'And the doctor? He has not proven to be a disappointment?'

They had poached Dr Gruber from the North Koreans, unbeknownst to them, of course. Sikes didn't object to making enemies. In her line of work it was unavoidable. But even Sikes drew the line at provoking a rogue state with nuclear capabilities and an army of over five million.

'The doctor is on track,' said Grimwig.

So, Sikes thought, everything was coming together nicely, minor hiccups apart. Talking of which, it was time Ollie Turner was dealt with, too. A single phone call should see to that.

As for all the other children locked away in that awful basement, there was no sense risking another escape. Besides, phase one was over. It was time to move on to phase two.

'The children,' Sikes said to Grimwig. 'I think it's time.'

'You mean . . .'

Bullseye was still licking his lips. Sikes lowered herself in front of him, so that she and the dog were nose to nose. As she tickled Bullseye behind the ears, she shut her eyes and breathed in, relishing the fresh scent of death. She exhaled and looked Grimwig in the eye.

'I mean kill them,' she said. 'Kill them all.'

16 NEW TOYS

'It's happening,' Jack said.

The investigations team was gathered in the control room. Keya was there, too. No one was particularly happy about inviting her into the Haven's nerve centre, but as they saw it they had no choice. Apart from anything they would need her help.

'Tell us,' said Dodge, as he and the others gathered around. Ollie stood slightly apart. He was fully committed to the fight now – if Maddy Sikes was involved, Ollie had more reason to get to the bottom of things than anyone – but he still felt like the new kid at school.

'The war Ollie predicted,' Jack explained. 'It's happening. Only skirmishes for the time being, but there are fights breaking out all over the city.'

Jack was monitoring Twitter, Ollie saw, as well as Instagram, Snapchat and several newsfeeds. Altogether there were three computer screens spread before her, and the third displayed what appeared to be an exact mirror of the police control system. Ollie knew from Nancy that all emergency-services communications were off limits to the general public. Jack must have hacked her way in.

She shrugged guiltily when she noticed Ollie looking.

'We try not to break the law if we can help it,' she said, 'but some information is too valuable not to use.' She tapped the screen. 'Stuff like this helps us save lives.'

Dodge was peering over Jack's shoulder, scanning the computer screens himself.

'You were right about your brother,' he said to Keya. 'There's a report of five police units called to a disturbance on the Winslow estate in Brixton. That's Southsiders' turf, right? Two officers injured, seven gang members taken to hospital. Sixteen people in custody.'

Keya looked worried. 'Does it say who was hurt? Does it give names?'

Dodge winced apologetically and shook his head.

'Danny Hunter's at it, too,' Flea said, prodding one of his fingers towards the screen in the middle. 'I guess he believed us that we didn't take his son. From the look of it he's blaming the Shiver Street Posse.'

'Who are probably blaming Danny Hunter for taking their own missing kid.' Jack scrolled through the newsfeed Flea had spotted. 'Your uncle Danny isn't messing around,' she said. 'Shiver Street's headquarters have been set on fire. Four fire engines on the scene. Reports of casualties, but no word on numbers.'

Ollie edged closer to Jack's desk. 'Wait. If he's blaming the Shiver Street Posse now, does that mean he'll let Erik go?'

'No chance,' said Dodge. 'Why would he? He doesn't *know* Shiver Street were responsible, but it's like Keya said: he can't afford to look weak, just in case they *did* take Harvey. And as far as he's concerned he's got us working for him for free. What's he got to gain by letting Erik go?'

Ollie stole a glance at the countdown on Dodge's watch. Already they had less than twenty hours until the midday deadline.

'There's another fire in Acton,' said Jack, scrolling on. 'More fights in Wandsworth, Islington, Chelsea. From the sound of it the emergency services are struggling to cope.'

'But what's Maddy Sikes got to gain by getting the city to tear itself apart?' said Sol. 'London is her turf, too. She doesn't own as much of it as she'd like to, but it's not in her interest for London to become a war zone. Surely it's got to be bad for business.'

'That all depends on what kind of business you're talking about,' said Jack.

'And that's the question,' said Dodge. He shook his head. 'What on earth is Sikes playing at?'

Ollie had been wondering the same thing himself. He'd been thinking about Nancy, too; about how ruthlessly Sikes had ensured she was out of the way. It made no sense that Sikes would murder a cop for no good reason, not unless that cop was on the brink of discovering something Sikes was desperate to keep hidden. And a gang war just didn't feel enough somehow.

'Maybe the war itself isn't the point,' Ollie said. 'Maybe the chaos is – the fact that the emergency services are so stretched. Maybe the fighting, the fires, they're a distraction.'

No one spoke. Even Ollie felt numbed by the implications. If he was right that whatever was happening now was a prelude to something else – a way to keep the police busy – it meant that whatever was coming was on another scale entirely.

Flea was the one to break the silence. 'What does it even matter?' he said. 'Who cares what Maddy Sikes is *planning*. The fact is we've found her out. We know she's behind this, whatever it is, so let's *do* something about it. Let's rescue those kids and get them home, and then the fighting will stop. After that happens, Sikes's scheme will be over before it's even begun.'

Lily moved closer to her brother. 'That's not such a bad idea, you know,' she said to Dodge. 'Whatever Sikes has in mind, there's no sense us waiting around for it to happen.'

Dodge frowned at the computer screens. He wasn't reading any more, Ollie realised. He was deciding.

He stood tall.

'Flea's right,' he announced.

Flea, in the background, let out a sigh of relief. 'Finally,' he muttered.

'We do what Flea suggested,' Dodge went on. 'We go back to the warehouse.' When Flea started to move, Dodge held up a finger. 'But just me, Keya . . . and Ollie.'

'*What?*' Flea blurted.

Even Ollie was surprised.

'We're the only three who know the layout,' Dodge reasoned. 'And if we all go, there's a greater chance we'll be spotted. Sikes will have heard about Keya's escape by now, which means her lookouts will have their guard up. We need to move quickly and stealthily. Below the radar. Agreed?'

Dodge was looking at Flea, who was the only member of the investigations team not to nod. Instead he was visibly fuming.

Dodge turned to Keya. 'Does that work for you?' he asked her.

'You bet it does,' Keya replied, a look of fierce determination in her eyes.

'What about you, Ollie?' said Dodge. 'Are you up for it?'

Ollie allowed himself the briefest glance towards Flea. 'When do we leave?' he said.

Only Flea refused to follow them into the kit room. He'd stormed off after Dodge had announced his decision, slamming doors in his wake.

Ollie tried to focus on the matter in hand, conscious he was heading to the very prison he'd just escaped from.

'Remember, Ollie,' Dodge told him, back in the kit room. 'This is a rescue mission. It's not the time to be thinking about revenge.'

Ollie looked up and for a moment held Dodge's gaze. Then he nodded.

'Before you go,' said Jack to Ollie, 'I've got a few little toys for you that might prove useful.'

She presented Ollie with a phone that looked exactly like Dodge's, right down to the modified antenna.

'It isn't fully loaded the way Dodge's is, but there are enough special features to keep you going. Most important is the comms app, which will work even down in those tunnels. Dodge will see all your messages on his phone, and we'll be able to monitor them at this end, too.'

Ollie took the phone in his palm. It felt heavier than a typical iPhone. The added weight was oddly reassuring.

'And there's one of these for you as well.' Jack held out a purple silicone wristband, the same colour as his old school uniform.

'It's nothing fancy. But hidden inside is a high-strength tracking device. There's one in your phone as well, obviously, but if you're caught your phone will get taken from you. Chances are a wristband will be overlooked. And even if it's not, it's impossible to switch the signal from these babies off, so at the very least we'll know where to start looking for you.'

Ollie wasn't reassured by Jack's talk of him being captured. He slipped the purple band around his wrist. For the first time he saw the other members of the investigation team were all wearing one, too, though each seemed to have a different colour. Jack's was yellow, for instance. Dodge's was white.

'Lastly, Ollie, because you haven't had a chance to learn how to kick butt the way Song can . . .' Jack said, reaching behind her. 'Something to give any bad guys who happen to mess with you a bit of a shock.'

Jack held out a pair of plain, silver bands, a bit like matching wedding rings.

'Jewellery?' said Keya, watching on. 'What are you gonna do, bling the bad guys to death?'

'Something like that,' said Jack, with a smile. She put the rings on, one on each hand. 'Touch something with one ring and nothing happens.' Jack held a ring against Sol's bare arm. 'But touch something that conducts electricity with *both* rings . . .' She reached with her other hand, but before she could make contact Sol leapt away.

'Uh uh,' Sol said. 'I'm not being your guinea pig for this one.'

Jack looked around for another victim, but everyone else took a step away from her, too.

'Spoil sports,' said Jack. 'It wouldn't have hurt *that* much. It'd feel like a large jolt of static electricity, that's all. Just enough to encourage whoever grabs you to let you go.'

She slipped off the rings and passed them to Ollie. 'One on each hand,' she reiterated. 'Then when you grab something – or someone – apply just a smidgen of pressure. Be warned, though: there's only enough charge to use them once.'

Ollie reached out nervously. He expected a shock when the rings touched his skin, but for some reason – the absence of pressure maybe? – they settled harmlessly in his palm. He fitted one on to each of his middle fingers. They were a little loose, but when he waggled his hands they didn't fall off.

'There's a set for you, too, Keya, if you want one,' said Jack. 'And I can rig you up a wristband, if you like.'

'Thanks, but no thanks,' said the girl, proudly. 'I know how to handle myself. And the last thing I want is someone – anyone – knowing exactly where to find me.'

'That's kind of what I thought you'd say,' Jack replied.

Ollie splayed his fingers in front of him, studying the inconspicuous-looking rings.

'All set then?' said Dodge, moving through the group. He stopped at the door that led down into the tunnels and faced back into the room.

'Be careful,' said Lily, edging forwards. Ollie saw her fingers interlink with Dodge's, and watched as she kissed him lightly on the lips.

A hand fell on Ollie's shoulder and he spun, feeling guilty. But it was only Sol, offering out his other hand for Ollie to shake.

'Good luck, mate,' Sol told him as he pumped Ollie's arm. 'And if you happen to run into Mad Maddy,' Sol went on, his anxious smile setting firm, 'you might want to remind her who she's messing with.'

17 LION'S DEN

They moved quickly through the tunnels, retracing the route of their escape. Long before Ollie expected him to, Dodge called them to a halt.

'Are we there already?' Ollie asked in a whisper.

'We're here,' answered Dodge. 'Right back where you and I started, Ollie.' He pointed, and Ollie recognised the ladder on the wall behind him.

'Won't they be expecting us to come in the same way we got out?' Ollie asked.

'Who says they know how we got out?' said Dodge. 'You closed the manhole cover behind you, right, Keya?'

'Course I did,' said Keya. 'And before you ask, no one spotted me heading down here either.'

Dodge bobbed his head approvingly, then peered up into the gloom. 'Besides,' he said, 'I doubt they'll be expecting us at all. We barely got away last time. After what we went through, surely we wouldn't be foolish enough to come back.'

Dodge showed Ollie a grin then, and Ollie couldn't help but return it. Even Keya responded with a roguish smile.

They climbed the ladder, Dodge first, then Keya, and finally Ollie. Dodge lifted the manhole cover carefully, a fraction at a time, and as every second passed, Ollie half expected a shout, a gunshot, to split the silence.

But none came, and once Dodge was sure the coast was clear, he clambered out into the courtyard. Keya and Ollie followed him.

The lorry that had been parked there before was still in place, giving them a welcome point of cover. It was growing dark, too, meaning it was already later than Ollie had assumed.

'Follow me,' Dodge instructed, 'and keep low.'

It wasn't like before. Ollie recalled the number of guards who'd been stationed in the grounds last time, the shouts of the men who'd been pursuing them. Now it was deathly silent, with no sign of anyone anywhere.

He should have been relieved, Ollie knew. So why was it he had the feeling that something was wrong?

As they approached the building, Dodge glanced back at him, and Ollie could tell from his expression that Dodge was worrying about exactly the same thing.

They knew better than to try to enter the warehouse through the fire door, so they searched for another way in around the back. They found one quickly: a window on the ground floor that was slightly ajar.

Too simple, Ollie told himself. *Surely this is far too simple.*

He posted himself through the gap and joined the others in a crouch on the warehouse floor.

The *empty* warehouse floor.

The window had led them into a corner of the enormous space, which before had been stacked with crates. It wasn't Maddy Sikes's usual sort of shipment, Dodge had said at the time, and Ollie had wondered what he meant. But it no longer mattered. Whatever Sikes had been transporting, it was already long gone.

After making sure they were alone, Dodge powered up the torch on his phone, and Ollie, beside him, did the same. Sweeping the beams across the concrete floor, they saw not a single empty box, nor even a discarded cigarette end. It was as though they'd imagined what they'd seen happening here last time, or somehow come to the wrong warehouse.

Dodge and Ollie shared a look.

'Well?' hissed Keya. 'What now?'

Ollie tried to ignore the voice in his head. *You're too late*, it told him. *You had a chance before, but now you've blown it. The kids are gone, Erik's gone, and Maddy Sikes – Nancy's killer – has got away. And it's your fault.*

Dodge turned off his torch. Ollie followed his lead. As their eyes adjusted to the darkness, Dodge rose from his crouch.

'We carry on,' he said, keeping his voice low, as though he trusted the empty warehouse as much as Ollie did. 'Nothing's changed. Just because the shipment's gone, doesn't mean they've moved the prisoners. And if they have, they can't have taken them far.'

Keeping tight to the wall, where the shadows were thickest, they started forwards. Ollie realised he was sweating, from the tension rather than the temperature. He wiggled his fingers, feeling the weight of the rings Jack had given him, and hoping the moisture in his palms wouldn't accidentally set them off.

All of a sudden, there was a *clonking* noise, and the warehouse floor was flooded with light.

'It appears some rats have managed to escape the sewer,' came a voice, as clear and cold as ice.

Ollie spun. He saw a woman, tall and sculpted in black, with a cloud of bristly white hair. She sparkled when she moved, her diamond jewellery refracting lasers of light.

Maddy Sikes, surely.

At her side was one of the biggest dogs Ollie had ever seen.

Unconsciously, Ollie took a step towards them. Rather than fear, all he felt at that moment was pure fury – a determination to make Sikes pay for what she'd done. But then Ollie noticed the guards who'd appeared around the room. There was a small army of them: twenty or thirty at least. Ollie and his friends were surrounded.

'Go!' Dodge said. '*Run*.'

He didn't need to tell them twice.

'Get them!' Sikes roared.

Dodge was sprinting towards a ladder maybe fifteen metres ahead. Ollie had no idea where it led. But if they managed to climb up and then kick the ladder away, they would at least buy themselves some time.

And they were out of options. Every other exit on the warehouse floor was blocked.

One of the guards, faster than his friends, was already barrelling into their path. He spread his arms as Dodge drew close, but at the final second Dodge rolled, bowling the guard to the floor.

Ollie had pulled ahead of Keya, and he managed to hurdle the guard where he lay. As he landed he drew level with Dodge, who was back on his feet.

They sprinted on, with Keya right at their shoulders, until abruptly she let out a scream.

As one, Ollie and Dodge turned. The guard Dodge had felled had somehow grabbed hold of Keya's trailing leg. Another guard was already upon her.

'Keya!' Ollie yelled. He turned, and made to go back to help their friend, but Dodge tugged him away. Just in time: a third guard had appeared from nowhere, and would have seized Ollie, too, if Dodge hadn't hauled him back.

'Go!' Keya yelled at them, and Ollie realised they had no choice.

Dodge spun away, dragging Ollie after him. The final few metres to the ladder were blocked by a freakish-looking man with a shark-like grin. Dodge accelerated, dipping his shoulder and driving right into the man's chest. The man tumbled from their path like a skittle, clearing the way to the bottom few rungs.

Dodge scrambled up the ladder first, and when he reached the platform he leant down and held out his hand.

'Faster, Ollie! They're closing!'

Ollie climbed as quickly as he could. Before he could stretch to clasp his friend's hand, however, someone seized hold of his foot.

Ollie didn't even bother to look. He kicked, and felt whoever was gripping him let go.

For a moment Ollie thought he would make it. He managed to get another rung higher, within reach of Dodge, but this time it was more than one hand that grabbed him. Ollie felt *both* his legs being seized, and when he looked he saw half a dozen guards at the bottom of the ladder, all fighting to drag him to the floor. It was like staring down at a pit of crazed zombies.

'Ollie!' Dodge shouted, and Ollie felt his friend's hand fasten around his forearm. For one elongated moment, Ollie was being pulled in two, a human rope in a vicious tug of war.

But there was never any doubt about which side would win. Dodge's hand slipped, until his fingers snagged around Ollie's wristband. For those final half seconds, it was only the strength of the silicone band that was keeping the two of them linked together.

But then the rubber snapped, and Ollie's wrist came loose, and he was falling . . .

Falling . . .

Towards the floor.

18 DEFCON ONE

There was nothing Ollie could do to fend them off. He was grabbed from all sides, and before he knew what was happening he was being carried roughly through the warehouse.

They threw him into a darkened room, and for a moment Ollie thought he was back behind the door he and Keya had escaped from. But then there was the sound of an engine – a big one, diesel – and the very walls began to vibrate.

He was in the back of a truck, Ollie realised. A *moving* truck. For the first time he noticed the temperature, a chill like he was shut inside a fridge.

There was a shuffling sound beside him, and Ollie narrowed his eyes to peer deeper into the gloom. Slowly a series of shapes began to emerge, too confused for Ollie to make any sense of them. But gradually the dark began to clear, and Ollie came to understand what he was looking at. Legs, feet, arms, heads: a sprawl of people at the far end of the container.

Ollie wasn't alone.

'Hello?' he said. He was half lying, half kneeling near the container's doors, in the spot where Sikes's guards had thrown him. He rose unsteadily to his feet and, using the walls of the truck to steady himself, made his way towards the cab end of the vehicle.

A voice filtered weakly through the darkness.

'Ollie? Is that you?'

Ollie paused and angled his head. 'Keya?'

'Over here, Ollie.'

Ollie continued another pace forwards, and then he saw her. And not just her. Keya was the nearest of maybe two or three dozen kids, all huddled together at the end of the container furthest from the lorry's rear doors.

The missing kids. Ollie had found them, if not quite perhaps in the way he'd imagined.

Keya was slumped against the wall. The only light in the back of the lorry seemed to be coming from a row of weak strip lights along the ceiling, a bit like the emergency lights in an aeroplane, but even in the dimness Ollie could see how badly Keya had been hurt. She was bleeding from her lip, and the area around her left eye was raw and swollen.

'They got you, too, then,' Keya mumbled weakly. She gave Ollie a bitter, defeated smile. 'I'd hoped you and Dodge had got away.'

She seemed to be trying to peer across Ollie's shoulder. Ollie turned to check where she was looking, then quickly scanned the faces of the other children.

'Dodge isn't here?' he said.

Keya flopped her head from side to side. 'Last time I saw him he was with you.'

Which meant ... what? That Dodge had indeed got away? Ollie felt a flicker of hope. If Dodge had made it out, that meant help might soon be on its way. Except then Ollie remembered what had happened, and his fingers touched his bare wrist. His tracker. The wristband. It had snapped when Dodge had tried to rescue him. His phone was gone as well, meaning the Haven crew had no way of locating him. And the lorry might be taking them anywhere.

Ollie turned to the other kids. None of them had so far said a word, and when Ollie looked closer he saw that nobody was moving. Some sat staring vacantly, but mostly their eyes were closed.

'What's wrong with them? Are they . . .'

'They're alive,' Keya told him. 'But they're freezing. Who knows how long they've been kept in here. I'm already turning blue and I've only been in here ten minutes.' As if to prove her point, Keya succumbed to a violent shiver. She was wearing a shirt, the sleeves ripped off at the shoulders, and Ollie could see the goose pimples on her bare skin.

'It must be a grocery lorry or something,' Ollie said. 'The kind supermarkets use.' He dragged his hoodie over his head. 'Here, take this.' He settled the jumper like a blanket on top of Keya.

The lorry gave a lurch then, and Ollie toppled against the container wall. He allowed himself to slide to the floor, huddling against Keya the way the other children had squashed together in their desperation to keep warm. He sat staring at their glassy eyes, saw one or two twitch as though they were dreaming . . . and then, whether from the cold or the motion of the lorry or simply from sheer exhaustion, Ollie found himself falling asleep, too.

He woke to a rumble from beneath him, and a sharp pain in his ribs.

'Wake up, Ollie. We're slowing down.'

Ollie's eyelids had a Monday-morning heaviness.

'What time is it?' he mumbled. 'Am I late for school?'

There was another sharp jab into his side. Ollie turned and saw Keya beside him. The shriek of brakes cut through him like an alarm, and Ollie jolted awake, reality splashing over him like cold water.

'What's happening?' he said. 'Where are we?'

Keya moaned as she slithered herself upright. 'I'm not sure. I must have fallen asleep at some point myself.'

She'd been right what she'd said before: the lorry was definitely slowing down. The change in the vehicle's movements, as well as the periodic howl of the brakes, was slowly rousing the other children, too.

A voice spoke out from close beside them. 'Who are you two? I didn't see you in here before.'

The girl who'd spoken was older than Ollie by two or three years. Her black hair was hanging in braids, with a different colour bead at the end of each one, and she had piercings on her ears, nose and lower lip. She was no more warmly dressed than any of the other kids, but unlike most of them she already appeared fully alert.

'Shiver Street cretins, I'd bet,' said a boy beside her, more groggily. Like the girl, the boy was about fifteen or sixteen. He had spiky hair, a sharp chin and a nose that jutted like an eagle's beak. He was wearing a baggy jeans/vest top combination that to Ollie looked immediately familiar.

'This is our corner, losers,' the boy went on. 'Go on, scram. The deadbeats' area is over there.'

'Shut up, Harvey,' the girl told him. 'We're past all that, don't you think? You heard what they plan to do to us. Seems a bit pointless fighting among ourselves when we're all sinking in the same boat.'

Ollie looked again at the boy. 'Harvey?' he said. 'Harvey Hunter?'

The boy tightened his already narrowed eyes. 'That's me,' he said. 'Who's asking?'

Before Ollie could reply, Keya spoke to the girl. 'What did you just say? *What* do they plan to do to us?'

The girl smiled grimly. 'We overheard a pair of guards,' she said. 'Not that they were bothering to keep their voices down. You ask me, they *wanted* us to hear.'

'But hear what? What did they say?'

'They're gonna kill us,' said Harvey Hunter. 'Murder us and dump our bodies all over London. Right out in the open, they said. In places we'd be found. Said we'd be making headlines by lunchtime.'

Ollie wasn't wearing a watch, but he saw one on the wrist of a smaller kid sitting nearby. It was coming up to four in the morning, according to the display. The kid who owned the watch, which was far too big for his wrist, seemed on the verge of tears. He was listening to every word Harvey Hunter and the others were saying.

'But . . . why?' Keya said. 'And if their plan was to kill us all along, why haven't they done it already?' She spoke to the girl with the braids, but turned to Ollie for an answer.

'Timing,' he said. 'That's the only thing that makes sense. The kidnappings were to get the war going. When bodies start showing up in gangs' territory, the entire city will go to DEFCON 1.'

'War?' said the girl with the braids. 'What are you going on about? Who's at *war*?'

Harvey Hunter slapped his knee with glee. 'My old man,' he said to Ollie. 'Right? I knew he'd go looking for me! I knew he wouldn't take it lying down! He's giving it to those Shiver Street wimps, am I right?' When he smiled at Ollie it was mainly a sneer.

'Shut *up*, Harvey,' said the girl, this time whacking him on the arm. 'By the sound of it your old man is part of the problem here. Isn't that right . . .' She looked at Ollie questioningly. 'What's your name, by the way? I'm Imani. Harvey you've met,' she added, with a disapproving curl of her lips.

'I'm Ollie. Ollie Turner. And this is Keya. We're . . .' Ollie hesitated, then pulled back his shoulders. 'We're with the Haven.'

He noticed Imani's eyes widen in silent awe, and he wondered whether she'd assumed the Haven was a myth the way Keya had.

'Not me,' Keya put in. 'Technically I'm a Forza. But me and the Haven lot, we're working together on this.' There was a note of pride in Keya's voice when she spoke, Ollie noticed, in contrast to the way she'd mocked the Haven crew back in the kit room. 'We came to rescue you,' Keya went on.

'Oh yeah?' sniffed Harvey, rubbing his arm where Imani had hit him. 'And how's that going, would you say?'

Before Keya had a chance to respond, the lorry braked sharply, and all the kids toppled into a bundle. There was a chorus of complaints – calls of 'Hey!' and 'Watch it!' and 'Get your armpit out of my face!' – before gradually they recovered their balance. Ollie pressed a palm to the wall, bracing himself for the lorry to start moving again.

Instead the engine cut off.

'We've stopped,' Imani whispered.

'You don't say,' Harvey hissed back.

The children sat waiting for something to happen.

After minutes that felt like hours, the door into the container swung open, and the darkness was split by a shaft of light. Ollie watched as the torch beam settled on the children across from him, passing methodically from face to face. It reached Imani, then Harvey, then Keya, then Ollie, then the boy with the watch, then . . .

The beam swung back to Ollie.

'That's him,' said a voice.

'You!' said another. The torch beam waggled to indicate Ollie, and in the flash of light Ollie saw that one of the men was holding a gun. 'Get over here. *Now*.'

Ollie hesitated, then staggered upright. Keya, beside him, rose too.

'*Just* you,' said the voice. 'The rest of you, stay exactly where you are.'

Keya and Ollie exchanged a look, then Keya sank slowly to the floor. 'Be careful,' she whispered.

Ollie started moving towards the doors. The closer he got to the end of the container, the lighter it became. Beyond the men who stood waiting for him was what appeared to be an underground car park.

'Get a move on, boy. We ain't got all day.'

As he drew closer to Sikes's guards, something caught Ollie's eye.

'Wait,' he said. 'I . . . I forgot something.' Abruptly Ollie turned and hurried back to where the others were sitting.

'Oi! Where are you going? Don't make us come in there and get you!'

Ollie squatted in the place he'd been sitting before. He looked at the kid who'd been crying. 'Your watch,' Ollie hissed. 'Give it to me.'

The boy withdrew his watch hand protectively. 'What? Why?'

'Just give it to him,' said Keya, although when Ollie looked across at her, she was clearly as puzzled as the boy was.

Reluctantly the boy passed Ollie his watch. Ollie looped it around his wrist, then turned again to Keya. 'Fill them in about what's been going on,' he instructed, gesturing with his chin to the kids around them. 'And then, after that, make sure they're ready.'

'But . . . what do you mean? Ollie, wait!'

Ollie was already halfway back towards the end of the container. He was about to turn, to say something more, when one of the guards grabbed him by the arm. The man tugged, yanking Ollie so hard he fell into the car park. Then the doors of the lorry slammed shut, leaving Keya and the others in the dark.

19 ARCH ENEMY

Ollie was half led, half dragged through the car park.

The men shoved him into a lift, and forced him to stand in one corner. One of the guards hit a button and the doors into the lift slid closed. They were going up, from what Ollie gathered. *All* the way up.

The lift hummed like the lifts on the USS *Enterprise*, and it was only because Ollie was paying close attention that he felt it moving at all.

In no time it arrived wherever it was taking them. There was a ping like a text message on a smartphone, and the doors glided gracefully apart.

Maddy Sikes was standing straight ahead.

She was maybe twenty paces from Ollie, in a vast room with a marble floor and floor-to-ceiling windows that overlooked the city below.

It was daybreak, and Ollie had never seen London looking so beautiful. They must have been two hundred metres in the air, level with the top of the tallest office buildings in the city. The sky was a freshly born blue, tinged with a dusting of pink.

Ollie knew the guards wouldn't have let him move if he'd wanted to, but in that moment he had no intention of going anywhere. The view captivated him. It took all his effort to shift his attention back to Sikes.

She was talking to a long, spindly man with almost no hair and a face so gaunt, Ollie could see the exact shape of his skull. Between them was a short, ugly man, who Ollie recognised from the warehouse. He'd been blocking their escape, Ollie remembered, before Dodge had knocked the man to the floor. Ollie was pleased to see a large bruise on the side of the man's face.

Sikes spotted the elevator doors open, but she made no move towards where Ollie and the guards were standing. She seemed focused for the time being on the skeleton-like man across from her.

'Thank you, Dr Gruber,' she was saying. 'You've worked wonders in a very limited amount of time.'

The man – Gruber – did not appear soothed by Sikes's words. 'I told you it was unnecessary for me to come here,' he replied, in an accent that reminded Ollie of Erik's, and reminded him too how rapidly their time to rescue him was running out. 'Everything was prepared before the shipment was sent,' Gruber went on. 'My being here only puts us both in greater danger.'

'There is no danger, Dr Gruber, I can assure you,' said Sikes. 'Any danger that might have existed has been eliminated.'

Ollie almost missed it, but Sikes's eyes definitely flicked his way. She was talking about Nancy, he realised. Whatever Nancy had been investigating, she'd come so close to uncovering the truth that it had got her killed.

Ollie felt his fingers curl, his jaw clamp so tightly it began to hurt.

'And besides,' Sikes went on, 'soon enough we shall both be out of the city. There's a car waiting for you downstairs, and come five p.m., I'll be on a private plane to the Caribbean. We've neither of us anything to fear.'

'That may be,' Gruber answered. 'But nevertheless I shall require double. Do you understand, Ms Sikes? Double the payment you promised me.'

'You will receive your just reward, Doctor, believe me,' Sikes replied, with a sly, slippery smile. She offered her hand for Gruber to shake, then extended her arm. 'Grimwig, why don't you show Dr Gruber the quickest way out?'

'With pleasure,' the ugly man – Grimwig – replied. He too held out an arm, gesturing for the doctor to go first. Dr Gruber nodded curtly to Sikes and, with a look of distaste directed towards Grimwig, headed off the way Sikes's assistant was showing him.

Finally, when Grimwig and the doctor were gone, Sikes turned her attention to Ollie. The guards had kept him trapped in the open lift, but now the man who'd been blocking the doors moved aside, and Ollie felt himself shoved from behind. He stumbled forwards, and his toe caught on the lift's edge, sending him sprawling to the floor. Before Ollie could recover himself, Maddy Sikes was standing over him.

'Come now, Ollie Turner,' she said. 'There's no need to grovel.' She bent close, and smiled at him sadly. 'Although I must say it does suit you. It's just a shame it isn't going to save you.'

As Ollie climbed to his feet, one of Sikes's guards gave him a boot in his ribs. Ollie might have fallen again, but this time he refused to go down.

Sikes moved off, and seated herself behind a desk the size of Ollie's old bedroom. The men positioned Ollie on the opposite side.

He raised his chin.

'You killed my friend,' he said to Sikes. 'And I'm not going to let you get away with it.'

For a moment Sikes just stared. Her eyebrows twitched, as though in confusion. Then she made a shrill, bird-type noise that sounded like nails being scraped down a blackboard. It took a moment for Ollie to identify the noise as laughter.

After that there was a growl, and when Ollie looked for its source, he realised it was coming from beneath the table. There, at Sikes's feet, was the dog Ollie had seen in the warehouse, the one the size of a wolf: a big one, a warg, like in *The Lord of the Rings*. Ollie couldn't help but focus on its teeth.

'My, my,' said Sikes, still chuckling. 'You are a chip off the old block, aren't you? And just like Detective Inspector Bedwin, you're proving to be something of a pain in the posterior. That's partly why I wanted to meet you before we dispose of you: to see whether you'd exhibit the same foolish stubbornness she did.' She caught Ollie's ferocious glare. 'And it seems I have my answer.'

Ollie couldn't bear to hear Sikes speak about Nancy with such contempt.

'Shut up!' he blurted. 'Don't you talk about her! Don't you even *dare*!'

Ollie found himself being knocked forwards. One of the guards had struck him across the back of his head, and Ollie would have fallen to the floor had Sikes's desk not stood in his way. His breath was driven out of him as his stomach collided with the edge of the table.

For several moments Ollie didn't move. He couldn't. But also, he dimly came to realise what he was staring at.

On the surface of the desk, spread out before him, was a map. It was upside down from Ollie's perspective, but he recognised London immediately. There were Xs dotted all over the city, maybe twenty of them in total. Each X was in the centre of an area that had been shaded a different colour, which

Ollie quickly realised corresponded with gang areas. 'Razors' read a handwritten note next to one zone. 'S. Street' read another. There were other names as well, ones Ollie didn't recognise. And there, in a spot in the east of the city, near a landmark Ollie knew well, was an asterisk beside a note saying 'Haven'.

Ollie felt his breath leave him a second time. She *knew*? Maddy Sikes knew where the Haven was? *How?*

Before Ollie could fully interpret what he'd seen, hands grabbed him around the shoulders. A guard was hauling him upright.

'Speak to me like that again,' Sikes said, 'and I'll ask Grimwig to deal with you the way he's currently dealing with Dr Gruber.'

Meaning what? That Gruber was about to be murdered the way Nancy was? *Show Dr Gruber the quickest way out*, Sikes had told Grimwig, and Ollie had visions of Gruber flying past the enormous window towards the street fifty storeys below.

He looked at Sikes with the same disgust she was showing him. It struck Ollie then how ugly she was. Not in the same way her assistant, Grimwig, was ugly. If Ollie had seen a photo of Sikes in a magazine, he would have assumed she was a famous actress or something. But it was like Nancy used to say: *Pretty people can be ugly, too, the same way those of us who will never be models can still be beautiful. It all depends on what you carry inside you. Or, more important, what it is that you allow to shine out.*

And Maddy Sikes, as Ollie looked at her, was projecting nothing but hate. Her beauty was skin deep at best. Not even that, really. It made Ollie think of make-up on something rotten.

'*Children*,' Sikes muttered, still exhibiting her evident distaste. 'If it were up to me you would all be drowned at birth. Or shut in cages like wild animals, until you came of age. Certainly you wouldn't be allowed to *speak* to anyone unless you demonstrated the proper respect.'

'Respect?' Ollie found himself echoing. 'What have you done to earn any respect? From *anyone*.'

For a second Ollie thought Sikes was about to lose it. She twitched as if, within, she were suppressing something like an earthquake. In the end, though, all she showed was that single tremor.

'That's just it,' she said. 'It's what I've *earned* that commands respect. What I *own*. There are very few people who can *afford* to disrespect me. And those who have, in the past, have already paid the ultimate price.'

Sikes's gaze seemed to turn inward. Her eyes had been grey before, like a churning sea. Now, unless Ollie was imagining it, they'd stilled to a subtle blue, as though whatever memory she'd been revisiting had calmed her.

'I must say,' she said to Ollie, 'I'm surprised you appear to have taken Nancy Bedwin's death so personally. From what I understand, you weren't even related. She was hardly *family*.'

She was goading him, Ollie realised. This time, he was determined he wouldn't rise to it.

'Talking of which,' Sikes went on, 'were you aware our paths had crossed before, Ollie Turner?'

Ollie frowned.

Sikes seemed to enjoy his evident confusion. 'I must say I was surprised when I realised myself,' she said. '*Amused,* rather.'

'What are you talking about?'

'Your parents,' Sikes said, and Ollie felt a wedge of something – an emotion like a physical mass – clog his throat.

Sikes leant back in her chair. Her dog had moved to her side, its blood eyes locked on Ollie, and Sikes sank her hand into its fur.

'I knew I recognised your name when I first heard it. And I never forget the names of my victims. They're like trophies to me, you see. I collect them. The way boys your age collect, I don't know –' she waved a hand dismissively – 'football stickers. Bruises.'

Ollie swallowed. He managed to clear enough space in his throat to allow him to speak. 'Victims?' he said. 'My mum and dad . . . they died in a terrorist attack. A bomb. That wasn't *you.*'

From being on the verge of losing her temper, Sikes was clearly beginning to enjoy herself.

'That's the other problem with children,' she said. 'You have no idea how the world works. You accept everything that happens at face value.'

Ollie was too focused on what Sikes was telling him to bother arguing. If he had, he would have insisted that Sikes had it backwards. That it was adults who so often overlooked what was really going on, and who refused to ever accept that they were wrong.

'In many ways it was your parents who set me on my path,' Sikes went on. 'Your parents and those who died with them. Without them, I wouldn't be the woman I am now, nor the woman I am about to become.'

She was talking in riddles, Ollie thought. Trying to confuse him into believing what she was saying. But she couldn't have been responsible for the death of his parents. She *couldn't*.

And yet, what possible reason would she have to lie?

'They were an experiment, you see,' Sikes said. 'A little taste of what this city has coming. A "terrorist attack" is what you called it, and that is just what I wanted the world to believe. Because there is nothing that inspires greater fear. And fear, Ollie Turner, is my friend. It's what I thrive on.'

Sikes leant forwards, eagerly, like someone who hadn't eaten for days who had just been served a gourmet meal.

'When people are afraid, they panic. And panic creates opportunity, for people who keep their heads. And staying calm is easy, if you know what's coming. If you're the one in *control*.'

Ollie was shaking his head. 'You didn't kill them,' he said. 'You *didn't*.'

Sikes's smile spread slowly, like a slick of something toxic.

'I'm afraid I did, Ollie Turner. It was my organisation that planted that bomb, on my orders. It was a practice run, you could call it, for what I'm planning to unleash now.'

Ollie didn't know when it had happened, but the guards either side of him had seized hold of his arms. Without consciously deciding to, he'd started forwards, to try to get at Sikes. But now he found himself pinned, looking at the woman who'd ruined his life through a blur of tears.

'I made you, Ollie Turner,' Sikes said, leaning back. 'I created you. Who you are, what you are, *where* you are. You're the person you've become because of me.'

Ollie was crying openly now. He couldn't stop himself. It was rage, anger, grief. And he was crying because there was nothing he could do.

'That's why you brought me up here?' he spluttered. 'To *gloat*?'

'I prefer to call it *reminiscing*. But yes, I wanted to see your face when you learned the truth.' Her smile became something resembling a sneer. 'Children like you have been trying to hurt me my whole life,' she went on, coldly. 'The bullies at that blasted boarding school. My so-called siblings. Vicious, evil creatures, every one of them. But in the end I beat them all.

Even your friends at the Haven, Ollie Turner, the ones who think they're so *good*. They're beaten, too, even though they don't yet know it.'

Through his tears Ollie saw Sikes stand.

'Take him back down,' she instructed her guards, all business now. 'Throw him in with the others. And when you dispose of him, make sure those Haven rats find his body. With any luck they'll blame that thug Danny Hunter, and start fighting among themselves like all the rest of them.'

Ollie felt himself being dragged away. Too late he started to struggle.

'You won't get away with it!' he yelled. 'Whatever it is, whatever you're planning, you won't win!'

The guards pulled him around, back towards the lift, so that Sikes was left standing behind him. He couldn't see her, but he could hear her all the same.

'My dear boy,' she said, laughing. 'I'm afraid I already have.'

20 SHOTS FIRED

Back in the underground car park, Sikes's guards shoved Ollie towards the lorry in which the others had been left waiting.

As Ollie was marched across the tarmac he noticed a fleet of ambulances lined up in the parking slots against the furthest wall. There must have been twenty of them in total. If Ollie didn't already know what was in the building above him, he would have assumed they were underneath a hospital.

Yet none of the ambulances appeared to be in use. The oddest thing about them was that they all looked brand new. And there was something else as well. Something Ollie, through his anger, couldn't quite put his finger on . . .

He had no time to contemplate further, because soon enough they were standing beside the lorry, in front of the double doors that would seal him inside. And if that happened, there was no way he would be getting out again. Not alive, at least.

Ollie hadn't forgotten about his plan. After his confrontation with Sikes, he was more determined than ever to make it work. But it was a half-plan at best, more reliant on luck than anything else. And on the hope that Keya had understood what he'd meant when he'd told her to ensure the others were ready, and that the others, in turn, had listened to her.

As one of the guards reached to open the container door, Ollie checked the watch on his wrist, the one he'd 'borrowed' from the boy inside. The watch had a steel strap, but didn't feel as heavy as it had initially looked. The label on the face said it was a Rolex, but even Ollie could tell it was a fake, something the little kid had worn to earn street cred. Ollie just hoped it was up to the job.

He unfastened the catch, so that the watch hung loosely on his wrist.

The right-hand door into the container swung open, and one of the guards stood ready with his gun. The children were all on their feet, but at the sight of the gun they shrank back.

At least they were standing, Ollie thought to himself. He'd half been expecting them to still be slumped against the furthest wall.

'Get inside,' instructed the guard who'd opened the door, and he shoved Ollie forwards.

As Ollie climbed he pretended to slip. He cursed, as though he'd hurt himself, and reached to haul himself up. The left-hand door to the container remained closed – the guards had only needed to open one side of the doors to throw Ollie back inside – and Ollie gripped the part where the catch on the open door would click into place when shut. As he did he allowed the watch to slip off his wrist, and he wedged it tightly into the cavity of the lock.

'Clumsy brat,' said the guard, and predictably enough gave Ollie another shove. Ollie was sent sprawling into the back of the lorry. When he landed it was right at Keya's feet.

'Ollie! Are you OK?'

Ollie winced away the pain of his landing. 'Are they ready?' he said, looking up.

'Yes, but . . . ready for what?' Keya hissed back.

Ollie turned, just in time to see the door into the lorry start to shut. He watched the light around its edge dwindle and then disappear completely, and when it did he was convinced his plan had failed. The watch had simply crumpled under the weight of the lorry door, and he and the others were shut inside until Sikes's guards came back to finish them off.

But then there was a grinding sound, like cogs that had become misaligned, and Ollie saw the doors hadn't closed properly after all. There was a tinkle of breaking glass – the watch face, Ollie assumed – and as the door rebounded Ollie saw something metal clatter to the floor.

The watch: it had come free. When the guard tried slamming the door again, there would be nothing to stop it latching in place. It was now or never.

Ollie sprang to his feet. 'Charge!' he shouted. '*Everyone!*'

Ollie was the first to reach the back of the lorry, but Keya and the others were right behind him. Against the tide of children breaking over them, the guards outside didn't stand a chance.

Ollie had to leap from the back of the lorry to avoid being crushed by the stampede. He clattered into the guard who'd drawn his gun, who toppled backwards, his weapon falling to the floor.

The second guard was on his back before he knew what was happening. The kids behind Ollie were on him, over him, and Ollie saw Keya pause long enough to rip the guard's gun from its holster and toss it away under the lorry. Ollie did the same with the gun the first guard had dropped, and then they were running, all of them, away from the overwhelmed guards and towards a strip of daylight Ollie spotted in the distance.

The way out, he thought. It *had* to be.

As they got closer Ollie saw a ramp leading up from the underground car park on to the street outside. Barring their way was just a single red and white barrier, which they could easily duck under or vault across.

Suddenly, from nowhere, more of Sikes's guards appeared, swarming from the shadows around them.

'Stop!' one yelled.

Ollie and the others veered away from the man who'd shouted, but two more guards appeared directly ahead of them, blocking their way to the ramp. One of them raised his weapon to his shoulder.

Ollie felt himself being yanked to one side just as the gun went off. He looked and saw Keya right beside him, pressed behind a concrete pillar. Wide-eyed, Ollie nodded his thanks.

The other kids were gathered behind them, having all dived for cover, too. There were more shouts, and Ollie saw that not only had Sikes's guards cut off their escape, there was another group closing from the rear.

'What now?' Keya said.

'*There*.' Ollie pointed across Keya's shoulder. Behind the row of parked ambulances there was an exit sign glowing green. Ollie's view was blocked by the line of vehicles, so he couldn't see the door beneath it, nor whether there was even a doorway there at all. But the ramp was blocked, and they couldn't head back towards the lorry, meaning the exit sign was their only chance.

'Go,' he urged, 'quickly!'

He and Keya started ushering the other children ahead of them, anxiously looking across their shoulders as Sikes's guards began to close in. Ollie saw one of them raise his weapon, but the man beside him swatted down the barrel before the first guard had a chance to fire.

'Are you crazy?' Ollie heard the man say. 'Look where you're aiming!'

But the man was aiming at Ollie. Wasn't he? He checked around, confused . . . and then he realised. The ambulances. The guard didn't want his colleague to fire at the ambulances.

'Get closer to the vehicles!' he called ahead, and tucked in tight beside an ambulance. He looked behind him and at least three of Sikes's guards were in a perfect position to shoot at him, but none did. Why? What was so special about a bunch of empty ambulances?

A sound made Ollie turn. It wasn't the guards this time, nor even the firing of a gun. What Ollie heard was something far worse.

It moved with terrifying speed: a blur of white charging through the shadows.

Sikes's dog. The warg.

Beyond it Ollie caught sight of Sikes herself, on the far side of the car park near the lifts. She was watching her pet's progress as intently as Ollie was, though in her case with anticipation rather than fear.

'Go!' Ollie said, shoving Keya forwards. 'Faster!'

Keya tried to turn, to see what they were running from, but Ollie kept driving her towards the exit.

They'd broken past the line of ambulances now, and there was indeed a door beneath the sign. Imani shoved it open and Ollie caught a glimpse of a staircase leading up. The panicked kids began to cram their way through. But the guards were closing – that *beast* was closing – and Ollie knew it was only a matter of seconds before they were caught.

Imani seemed to realise the danger, and frantically she began to urge the children on. 'Hurry!' Ollie heard her saying. 'And someone find something to barricade the door!'

They could all hear it now: the slobbering, snuffling snarl of Sikes's dog. When Ollie looked again it was close enough that he could see its salivating grin.

Now it was just Imani, Harvey Hunter, Keya and Ollie left outside. Harvey dived through the doorway first, shoving Imani out of his way.

'Jump, Ollie!' someone shouted. 'It's behind you!'

Ollie tried to do exactly that. He leapt, towards Keya's and Imani's outstretched arms, but as his fingertips brushed Keya's, his ankle suddenly caught fire.

Ollie screamed in pain, and he felt himself being dragged away from his friends across the floor. He wriggled, writhed, but fighting only made the pain worse. Sikes's dog had its teeth in Ollie's ankle, and it was tugging him back towards its master.

Ollie heard Keya yell and rush forwards to try to help him, but a bullet hitting the wall drove her back.

'Go!' he shouted through his agony. 'Just *go*!'

Another shot rang out and this time Ollie heard a scream. He couldn't tell if anyone was hit, but he sensed his friends dive for cover in the doorway.

Ollie kicked out with his other foot. His heel made contact with the dog's jaw, but if anything the blow only made it bite down harder. He tried kicking again, missed, and instead flailed helplessly with a fist.

And then he remembered. The rings. *Something to give any bad guys who happen to mess with you a bit of a shock*, Jack had said.

Ollie reached with his right hand and grabbed hold of the dog's left ear. Its eyes swivelled furiously, but there was nothing it could do, not unless it first let go of Ollie's ankle.

Grabbing hold of the other ear was trickier. The dog kept shaking its head, tearing at Ollie's leg. Ollie grabbed, missed. He saw a shadow closing over him, one of Sikes's guards, and he knew he had one final chance. He swung his hand – blindly, because his eyes were screwed up in pain – and felt his fingertips sink into something soft. *Apply just a smidgen of pressure*, Jack had said, but Ollie found himself pressing down with all his might.

A buzz ran through him like a shiver, but Sikes's dog felt it more than Ollie did. It let go of Ollie's ankle instantly, and leapt back so violently, it tripped up the approaching guard. The man fell, and would have collapsed on top of Ollie, had hands not seized him underneath each shoulder. For a moment Ollie assumed he was caught, but instead he was being dragged the way he'd been running: towards the exit sign, and the open door, which slammed shut the moment he was through.

21 SUGAR RUSH

Ollie lay sprawled at the bottom of the concrete stairs. Keya was leaning over him, anxiously surveying his wounded leg.

There was a thud from the garage side of the door, and a rattling sound as someone tried the handle. Imani had wedged a broom she'd found underneath it. 'This isn't going to keep them out for long,' she said.

Ollie shuffled until he was sitting. 'I heard a scream,' he said, 'after a gunshot. Did someone get hit? Is anybody hurt?' He checked Keya, who didn't appear to be harmed, and then Imani. The other kids had already disappeared up the stairs.

'You're the only one who was hurt,' said Imani. 'The scream was Harvey, but he wasn't hit. Just a bit afraid of loud noises, apparently.' She rubbed her shoulder where Harvey had barged past her. 'That boy can move, though, I'll give him that. Never mind who's standing in his way.'

The door shook again. The broom was holding, but only just.

'Can you walk?' Keya asked Ollie.

Ollie took hold of her outstretched hand and allowed her to heave him up. 'I'm going to have to,' he said.

They hobbled as rapidly as they could up the concrete staircase, Ollie's arm slung over Keya's shoulder. 'You're going to need stitches, Ollie. As well as a new pair of trousers.'

'What *was* that thing?' Imani asked from behind them. 'It looked like a . . . like a polar bear or something.'

'That was Sikes's pet,' Ollie answered, cringing from the pain of walking, and trying hard not to burden Keya with too much weight. 'A warg.'

'A what?'

Ollie shook his head. 'Never mind. I tell you something, though, I'd take my chances with a polar bear over that thing any day of the week.'

The staircase emerged directly on to an empty side street, in a part of the city Ollie didn't recognise. The street was narrow, with featureless office blocks on either side.

The other kids were gathered on the strip of pavement.

'We need to keep moving,' Ollie announced, hobbling with Keya and Imani into the centre of the group. He looked uneasily at the door they'd just come through, but there was no sign of anybody following them. 'There's no way Sikes will dare to chase after us in broad daylight, but the more distance we put between us and her the better.'

'Huh,' said Harvey Hunter, stepping forwards and shoving some of the smaller kids out of his path. 'I say we chase after *her*. Go for reinforcements, then come back here and finish what

190

she started. *Nobody* messes with a Hunter in this town and gets away with it.'

'Look out, Harvey!' said Keya suddenly. 'Maddy Sikes, she's right behind you!'

'What? Where?' Harvey leapt as though he'd been scalded, diving behind Imani for cover.

The rest of the group started laughing before Harvey realised he'd been tricked. He was clutching Imani's arm, and she brushed him off disgustedly.

'I say we tie Harvey to a lamp post,' she said. 'If Sikes wants him, as far as I'm concerned she can have him.'

'Works for me,' Keya said.

Harvey looked too angry – and too ashamed – to speak.

'He's coming with us,' said Ollie, even though he wasn't exactly thrilled at the prospect. 'I need him. Danny Hunter took one of my friends. Rescuing Harvey was the price Danny set for getting him back.' And the deadline was almost upon them, he didn't add. It was already morning, meaning Erik only had a few hours left.

'Come on,' Ollie said. 'Let's get moving.'

'But *where*?' said Imani. 'I don't even know where we are *now*.'

Ollie wasn't one hundred per cent sure where they were himself, nor in which direction they should be heading. But he recalled the markings on the map in Sikes's office, and he knew from the position of the rising sun which way was east.

'We go home,' he said, and he looked around at the lost and frightened kids. 'All of us. Together. We go to the Haven.'

Ordinarily a thirty-strong group of filthy and famished-looking kids skulking along the streets of London – with the boy who appeared to be their leader dripping blood along the pavement with every step – would have attracted exactly the sort of attention Ollie and the others were desperate to avoid. Fortunately, however, it was early, and the streets were deserted.

Once they'd escaped the maze of office blocks, Ollie was able to get his bearings. He gauged the distance to the London Eye on the horizon, and realised they had even further to travel than he'd hoped. The Haven was a two-hour journey by foot, Ollie reckoned, assuming the mark on Sikes's map was accurate. He was managing to walk without Keya's assistance now, but the way his leg felt, he wasn't convinced he would be able to make it.

The others were flagging as well, especially some of the younger kids. It was no wonder. They were hungry, thirsty and utterly exhausted.

Ollie called a halt as the group cut through a cobbled courtyard, a medieval patch of London that had been swallowed up by the modern sprawl. They were still deep in the city's financial district, with little except office blocks around them, but across the road Ollie had spotted a small, twenty-four-hour convenience store.

'Anyone got any money?' he said.

He turned out his pockets and found an old balled-up tissue and a twenty-pence piece.

'I've got a fiver,' said Keya, pulling a note from her sock. 'What?' she added, when she saw the way Ollie was looking at her. 'If I don't keep my money hidden, my brother'll just nick it to spend on fags.'

'I've got . . . seventy-eight pence,' said Imani, holding out some coins in her palm.

Both girls added what they had to Ollie's meagre offering.

'What about the rest of you?' Keya asked, and she began moving from person to person, gathering up whatever people were able to contribute. Most of the kids chipped in something, even if it was only a couple of coins. When Keya got to Harvey, Ollie noticed, Danny Hunter's son scowled at her, and kept his arms firmly folded across his chest.

By the time Keya was finished, they had a decent enough haul. Ollie did a quick headcount, and then took Keya and Imani with him to go shopping.

'Twenty-seven Mars Bars, please,' he said to the man behind the counter in the convenience store. 'And twenty-seven cans of Coke.'

'Make mine a Sprite,' said Imani.

'Twenty-six cans of Coke, one can of Sprite,' Ollie amended.

'And some Savlon,' chipped in Keya. 'And also a bandage if you have one.' She looked at Ollie. 'We might as well patch up that leg of yours if we're stopping.'

The man in the shop stared at them, until Ollie dumped the money on the counter. The man checked it, dropped it into the till and went to fetch a large box of Mars Bars from the back.

As Imani passed out the provisions back in the courtyard, Keya set to tending Ollie's leg. He winced as she wrapped the bandage, scrunching his eyes, and when he opened them again he saw they had company. The boy who'd given up his watch to Ollie had sidled over from the rest of the group.

'Thanks,' he said to Ollie. 'For saving us.'

Ollie was at a loss for what to say. He hadn't really thought about it like that.

'You're welcome,' he answered. 'Thanks for, you know. The thanks.'

The boy nodded. He sipped his Coke at Ollie, then turned away.

He spun back again. 'But you still owe me a new watch,' he said.

Kneeling on the floor in front of Ollie, Keya laughed. She tugged on his bandage, tightening it, so that all Ollie could manage was a muffled yelp. When he looked up, the boy had already faded back into the group.

The sugar had the desired effect. The kids regained some of the colour they'd lost while they'd been huddled in the refrigerated lorry, and nobody complained when Ollie signalled it was time to move.

Ollie felt better, too. Keya's first-aid skills had helped. His leg still hurt, but it had stopped bleeding, and the stabbing pain of each step had been replaced by a duller, more bearable throb.

He picked up the pace he'd set before, and again there were no complaints. The others were as keen as Ollie was to reach their destination.

The closer they got, however, the more the excitement turned to unease. They began to see signs of the war that had been breaking out across the city, which until now Ollie had only glimpsed through Jack's computer screen. They didn't come across any fighting themselves, but they heard sirens in the distance. It was a constant wail, like a baby crying in a neighbour's house. And there were plumes of smoke in almost every direction. Some were thin, half-hearted wisps. Others were thick, black columns, so dense they appeared to be holding up the sky.

Ollie couldn't help feeling anxious for another reason, too. They were drawing nearer to the spot that had been marked on

Sikes's map, but what if the map was wrong? Or what if it was right, but Ollie couldn't find the building they were looking for? He'd never seen the Haven from street level before. How would he be able to spot it? According to Aunt Fay, it was just another London building. *Entirely unremarkable*, was how she'd put it.

As they passed the Tube station Ollie had been aiming for, he slowed their pace to an amble. The city was steadily waking up around them, and already their ragtag fellowship had attracted a few inquisitive stares. People were uneasy, Ollie guessed, because of all the fighting. Someone was bound to challenge them sooner or later.

Entirely unremarkable . . .

There was a Subway on the corner, next door to a Starbucks; that was fairly unremarkable, at least for London. There was a parade of shops, a modern building that might have been flats and a beautiful old church. To Ollie's mind the church in particular was the exact opposite of unremarkable, but how was he supposed to tell? The Haven, on the inside, had seemed old, too, but maybe the outside was different. Maybe *that* was part of the building's camouflage.

As Ollie searched, he became aware of the grumblings that had sprung up around him.

'What's the hold-up?'

'So where is it then?'

'I told you he was lying – he's no more from the Haven than I am.'

'Why are we wasting our time? It's a myth, I tell you. A fairy tale.'

Keya was doing her best to quell the discontent, but even she was looking at Ollie with obvious concern.

But it was no good. He couldn't find it. None of the buildings on the streets around them appeared more likely to be the Haven than any other.

After the third time circling the same block, Ollie was on the verge of giving up. The map was wrong. Sikes was wrong. He should have been relieved that the Haven's secret was safe, but instead Ollie only felt sick. He'd lost them. Dodge, Sol, Lily. Jack, Song. Aunt Fay. Even Flea.

And Erik, of course. The deadline Danny Hunter had set was barely two hours away, meaning if Ollie failed to get Harvey back to the Haven soon, Erik was as good as dead.

But then Ollie noticed something on the building directly across the street. For a moment a bus blocked his view, and when it moved on Ollie scampered across the road to get a better look.

'Public Library' read the inscription he'd spotted. The words were faded but legible, and had been etched in a lintel above what might have once been a doorway, but was now a solid wall.

The building itself was made of pale grey stone, long dirtied by the pollution of the passing traffic. At first glance it appeared entirely featureless, but the closer Ollie studied it, the more ornate he realised the building was. It looked like a foreign embassy or something, but one that had long been standing empty. And somehow it seemed to fade into the buildings either side of it, which is why Ollie had missed it the first time. And the second. And the third. It was like that famous picture of a staircase that loops in a circle, which somehow manages to lead up as well as down. It was an illusion, in other words. It was camouflaged so effectively that even Ollie, who'd been looking for it, hadn't seen the Haven was there.

And a library. It made perfect sense, given how the building was laid out inside. Hadn't Ollie, the very moment he'd first entered from the sewer, detected the faint smell of books? The scent must have seeped into the plasterwork over the years.

'This is it,' he announced, as much to himself as to anyone else.

'Are you sure?' Keya was standing right beside him. Everyone was. Ollie hadn't noticed them follow him across the road.

Ollie smiled. 'I'm sure.' He lifted his chin, marvelling at the building. He couldn't see it – he couldn't see anything through the subtly shaded windows – but up there somewhere was Aunt Fay's secret garden. And just a few metres away, on the other side of the walls, were his friends.

'So how do we get in?' said Imani. She was looking where Ollie was, at the building's seemingly impenetrable facade.

Now Ollie's smile dipped. He looked left, right, up, down – and realised he had no idea.

22 DR GRUBER

As it turned out, they didn't need to worry.

'Ollie!'

Before Ollie could turn to the sound of the voice, he found himself staggering under the weight of a sudden embrace.

'You made it!'

'Lily?'

He couldn't see her through the onslaught of hair, which was somehow in both his eyes and his mouth, but he recognised the sound and smell of her. It was either her shampoo or her conditioner or *something* anyway that always surrounded Lily with a delicious scent of strawberries.

Ollie allowed himself to enjoy the moment, until he noticed Keya looking at him oddly, as though he'd done something wrong.

Before he had a chance to work out what, a hand landed on his shoulder and pulled him round. All at once instead of Lily it was Sol hugging him. Sol didn't smell as good as Lily did, but Ollie was just as delighted to see him.

'How did you get away?' Sol asked him as he squeezed. 'Dodge said you'd been captured!'

Ollie's grin dropped into something more uncertain. 'Dodge?' he said. 'Does that mean . . . he made it back?'

Throughout their trek across London, Ollie had barely dared to hope. He checked Sol's expression, fearful of what he would see there, but his friend's smile didn't alter. Rather, he gestured with his eyes. Ollie turned . . .

And there he was. Dodge was standing behind Lily, seemingly as amazed to see Ollie as Ollie was to see him.

'Ollie, I . . . I'm so sorry. I tried to save you, but . . . there were too many of them, and I . . . I just—'

Ollie cut him off, throwing his arms around his friend. When Dodge hadn't shown up in the back of the lorry, Ollie had known there was a chance he'd escaped. But there had been another possible explanation as well: that, if Dodge hadn't been captured, he'd been killed trying to get away.

'Well, ain't this sweet?' came a voice. 'It's like a scene in some soppy Hollywood romcom.'

Ollie and Dodge moved apart.

'Who's this?' said Dodge, his eyebrows arrowing in the middle.

Ollie smiled ruefully, almost like an apology in advance. 'This is Harvey Hunter,' he said. 'Danny Hunter's missing son.'

'And clearly a chip off the old block,' said Sol.

Harvey seemed at first to take Sol's comment as a compliment, then glowered when he realised it was the opposite.

'Watch it, Sonic,' said Harvey, mocking Sol's hedgehog-y dreadlocks. 'No one insults a Hunter in this town and gets—'

'Oh, put a sock in it, Harvey,' interrupted Keya. 'Don't you get tired of spouting the same old lines? Because I'm definitely getting tired of hearing them.'

Sol did his best to suppress a smile. 'Good to see you, Keya,' he said. 'Thanks for bringing our boy back in one piece.'

'Actually,' said Keya, 'it was more like the other way round. It was Ollie's quick thinking that saved the rest of us. If it hadn't been for him, we'd all be human icicles by now. You're lucky to have him,' she added, her eyes meeting Ollie's and then rebounding.

'You'll have to tell us all about it,' Dodge said to Ollie. 'Once we get you inside.' He gestured discreetly to the building behind them.

'How did you even know we were out here?' Ollie asked.

'Oh, you know Jack,' Dodge answered with a wink. 'She's got eyes everywhere.'

Ollie searched about for a hidden camera, but wasn't surprised when he couldn't find one.

'Come on,' said Dodge. 'This way.'

He led off, but Ollie made no move to follow him. 'Dodge?' he said. 'I know the rules, but . . . what about everybody else? You are going to let them in – aren't you?'

The other kids were gathered in a huddle. Now that they'd reached their destination, Ollie could see that they were overwhelmed with exhaustion.

For a moment Dodge appeared torn – eager to protect the Haven on the one hand, aware of how desperate the kids looked on the other.

'They're welcome,' he said at last. 'Of course they are. We'll take them in the back way, use their tops to blindfold them once we're down in the tunnels. Although to be honest they look so tired, they probably wouldn't remember the route anyway.'

Dodge led the company down an alleyway, and into the graveyard of the church Ollie had noticed before. Here, in a corner of the plot that at first glance appeared completely overgrown, there was an entranceway hidden beneath a gravestone that led down into the sewers.

Jack, Song and Flea were waiting for them when they reached the kit room.

'Sol, take our guests to the infirmary, would you?' said Dodge, indicating the bedraggled, wide-eyed children, who were removing their makeshift blindfolds. 'And then come and join us in the control room. Harvey, you stick with me. And don't get too comfortable – you won't be staying long. You might want to come along as well, Keya. We've got a lot to talk about.'

'And me,' said Imani. 'Whatever you lot are planning, I want in on it, too.'

Dodge looked at Ollie, who nodded. Dodge offered Imani his hand. 'Any friend of Ollie's is a friend of ours.'

Up in the control room, they waited for Sol before they began. Barring Erik, everyone from the investigations team was there, as well as Keya, Harvey and Imani. They gathered around the map table. Harvey was the only one to sit.

'First things first,' said Dodge. 'As soon as we're finished here, we get Harvey back where he belongs and exchange him for Erik. Danny Hunter gave us until midday, which means we've got –' he checked his watch – 'just over two hours left.'

'Me and Lily'll take him,' growled Flea. 'I wanna be there to hear Danny Hunter apologise. It'll be like seeing Halley's Comet or something, the sort of once-in-a-lifetime experience you tell your grandkids about.'

'Hunters don't apologise to anyone,' retorted Harvey. 'Not *ever*. It's part of our code.'

'Yeah, well, this time Uncle Danny's gonna have to,' Flea responded. 'At least if he wants to see his son again. What do you reckon, *cousin*? Does he love you enough to break his golden rule?'

Harvey swallowed, and his eyes skittered uncertainly around the room. Unexpectedly, Ollie felt a flash of sympathy for him.

'I appreciate the offer, Flea,' said Dodge, getting back to the matter in hand, 'but I'm going to give this one to Song. Erik's life is at stake. We can't afford for anyone – on either side – to lose their temper.'

Flea seemed about to argue, but stopped himself. Ollie guessed he'd realised that doing so would basically prove Dodge's point.

'Take some backup when you go, Song,' Dodge instructed. 'Three or four of your best students from the dojo.'

'Most of my best students are in this room,' said Song, 'but there are some brown belts in the intermediate class who could do with being put through their paces. I'll take them.'

So Song was the Haven's karate instructor, Ollie realised. He was surprised he hadn't worked it out before.

'Good,' said Dodge. 'Now that's settled, let's get back to trying to figure out what the hell Maddy Sikes is up to.'

Apparently this was Ollie's cue. He filled the others in on everything that had happened since the moment Dodge's hand had slipped from Ollie's wrist and Ollie had been captured in the warehouse. He told them everything he remembered, including what Sikes had revealed about her role in the death of Ollie's parents. He spoke quickly, almost mechanically, because he didn't want the emotion he was feeling to carry through in his voice.

By the time he was done, the control room had fallen quiet. There was just the gentle whir of the computer fans, and the background hum of the rest of the Haven going about its business. Someone was laughing on the floor below, and Ollie found himself envying anyone carefree enough to be able to do so.

Sol was the first one to break the silence. And, predictably enough, he said exactly what Ollie wanted to hear. 'We'll get her, Ollie. Don't you worry about that. One way or another, Maddy Sikes is going *down*.'

Without anyone noticing, Jack had rolled across to a computer screen. 'Ollie?' she said. 'Is this him? The man you mentioned. Dr Gruber.'

Ollie crossed to where Jack was sitting. On her computer screen was a black and white image of the man Ollie had seen in Sikes's office. The shot was fuzzy, as though it had been captured from CCTV footage, and enlarged further than the resolution would allow. Even so, Ollie recognised the shape of the man's head, the bony protrusions of his skull.

'That's him,' he confirmed.

'Dr Kurt Gruber,' said Jack. 'This is the only photo of him that I can find. The man is as elusive as the Loch Ness monster. He's a scientist, apparently. Born in Graz, Austria, educated at Cambridge University. Worked for the British government for a time, but then completely fell off the grid. He's wanted in thirty-seven countries, it says here. I'm not sure why, though. I can't seem to find anything about—' Jack stopped talking mid-sentence. She'd been firing words into Google, flicking from one search result to another, but as her computer screen settled on a page, her fingers ceased moving. She looked around, and Ollie watched the colour drain from her face.

'Jack?' said Lily. 'What is it? What have you found?'

Lily was afraid, Ollie realised. He could hear it in her voice. And he felt it himself: an icy chill channelling through his veins.

Jack cleared her throat. 'He builds . . . he builds bombs,' she said.

For a moment there was another stunned silence.

'Bombs?' Sol echoed. 'As in . . .'

'As in *big* ones,' said Jack. 'Chemical ones. The kind that release poison gas.' Her eyes fixed on Ollie. 'That man you saw, Ollie? Maddy Sikes's new best friend? He's an expert in weapons of mass murder.'

23 END GAME

'What else can you tell us about him, Jack?' Dodge had moved forwards. He was leaning on the desk, his weight on his fists. 'Jack?' he repeated.

'I . . .' Jack forced her fingertips back to her keyboard. She typed, scanned, typed again, and all the while sat shaking her head. 'Almost nothing,' she said, defeated. 'It's like I said, Gruber went completely off the grid. There are rumours he was working for the North Koreans, mainly because the last verified sighting of him was in Changchun, China. At least before Ollie saw him in Sikes's office.'

'Changchun?' Dodge echoed.

'It's in Jilin province,' Jack said. 'Right on the North Korean border.'

Dodge looked where Jack was pointing, at a map that was showing on her screen. His neck bulged as he swallowed.

He turned to Ollie.

'Those boxes,' he said. 'In Maddy's warehouse. Do you remember?'

'Only that they were there the first time,' Ollie answered, 'and they were gone when we went back. And you said . . .'

Ollie's eyes tightened. 'You said something about the shipment being unusual.'

Dodge nodded. 'Maddy Sikes isn't above a bit of smuggling,' he said. 'But I'm talking stolen art, weapons, diamonds. High-value stuff, always. But those boxes . . . according to the labels they were filled with toys.'

'Toys?'

'Right,' said Dodge. 'But the point isn't what was *in* the boxes. The point is what was *on* them. The labels – Changchun was the point of origin. That's where all those boxes came from. The same place anyone last saw Gruber.'

'Meaning . . .?' prompted Sol.

'Meaning there was more in those boxes than just toys,' said Jack, catching on. 'Meaning Gruber developed some sort of chemical weapon, probably while based in North Korea, and Sikes used that shipment to smuggle it into London.'

'And now it's gone,' said Dodge. 'Whatever Sikes has, whatever Gruber made for her, we've got no way any more of ever finding it.' He spun away from Jack's desk. 'She's mad. I never really believed it before, but she is. She's totally, utterly *insane*.'

'So that's her plan?' said Lily. 'To detonate some chemical weapon, right in the heart of the city?'

'More than one weapon, I'd bet,' said Dodge, turning back. 'That shipment Ollie and I saw was *huge*. And it only takes a small amount of chemicals to make a single bomb. Right, Jack?'

'Right,' said Jack, grimly.

'But *why?*' said Lily. 'And how is any of this connected to the missing kids? Why bother kidnapping anyone at all if ultimately she plans to kill . . . what? Hundreds of people?' She was looking at Jack for confirmation, but Jack's expression told her she was way off mark. 'Thousands, then?' she amended. '*Tens* of thousands?'

Jack dipped her eyes towards the floor. Lily wrapped a hand across her mouth.

'To create a diversion,' Ollie said, in answer to Lily's question. 'Those weren't just any kids she captured, remember? They were gang members. Important ones. And all from rival groups. And she meant to kill us. Dump our bodies all over London for Danny Hunter and the rest of them to find, at which point this war that's started would have escalated to Armageddon.'

'Meaning the entire police force would have been kept busy trying to restore order,' said Sol. 'Even busier than they are now, I mean. What's the situation, Jack? Have things calmed down at all?'

Jack was already shaking her head as she switched between windows on her computer screen. 'It's not quite Armageddon out there, but if anything it's worse than it was before. No one's backing down. The fights are intensifying, the fires are getting worse.'

'So Sikes has got all the cover she needs,' said Lily. 'She didn't even *need* to kill the kids.'

'No,' said Ollie. 'For Sikes, killing us would simply have been a bonus. She collects lives, you know. She told me.'

Ollie heard the hatred in his voice. It seemed to shock the others as much as it did him.

'So Maddy Sikes has got her hands on a bunch of bombs,' said Keya. 'We don't know how many, but we're guessing she's planning to set them off all across the city. Right?' She looked at the others for confirmation. 'So what exactly are we supposed to do about it?' she pressed. 'How can we stop the bombs going off if we don't even know where Sikes plans to plant them?'

Nobody had any answers.

'We do know,' said Ollie, and all eyes turned towards him. 'Think about it,' he went on. 'This war Sikes started, it's not just to keep the authorities busy. It's to ensure there's no one around after the bombs go off to challenge her. If she plants the bombs where the fighting is thickest, she eliminates her rivals and half the police force in one go.'

'At the same time as covering her tracks,' Jack chipped in. 'Set off a bomb in a war zone, and the authorities will be picking over the debris for years. Forensically speaking it will be a mess: a jigsaw puzzle of a billion pieces, none of which match any of the others. There'll be nothing to link the bombs back to Sikes.'

'The ambulances!' Imani announced. She'd so far been following the discussion in horrified silence. 'Remember, Ollie? In the car park? They didn't want to shoot at them. And I'm betting those bombs were the reason why.'

Ollie nodded. 'That's how she's getting the bombs around the city. In vehicles that everyone in the streets will immediately let through, because they'll think they're on their way to save people.'

'There was an entire row of them, though,' said Imani, appalled. 'There must have been fifteen, twenty ambulances at least.'

'Twenty-two,' said Keya. 'I counted.'

There was a silence as the group processed the implications. Twenty-two ambulances meant twenty-two bombs. Twenty-two sets of victims.

'Jack,' said Dodge. 'How would those bombs be set off?'

'It's hard to say,' Jack answered. 'The simplest solution would be to give each bomb an individual timer, and program them all to go off at the same time. But it would be easy enough to link them all to a central detonator. A laptop or a phone would do the trick. Anything capable of transmitting a signal.'

'Knowing Maddy Sikes,' said Sol, 'I'd bet money she'd want her finger on the trigger. For her it's all about control.'

The others grimaced their agreement.

'When, though?' said Lily. 'She must have a specific time in mind, even if she plans to be the one to press the button.'

'Today,' answered Ollie. 'It has to be. It's . . . what? Just after ten a.m. now. If everything had gone to schedule, the war Sikes started would have been raging by the middle of the afternoon. She'd have been planning to detonate the bombs when the rioting was at its peak.'

'Nightfall, then?' suggested Lily. 'That's when things will be at their worst, isn't it?'

'Except she'll also want to maximise casualties,' said Dodge.

'Rush hour, then,' said Jack. 'Five p.m., give or take.'

'Sikes mentioned something about being on a private plane by five p.m. when she was talking to Gruber,' said Ollie. 'It *has* to be then.'

Meaning they had less than half a day to disrupt Sikes's plan.

'What I still don't understand is *why*,' said Lily. 'What's Sikes's end game? So she eliminates her rivals, decimates the police. What's the point if she destroys half the city while she's at it? She'll be king of the castle, but her kingdom will be nothing more than a pile of rubble.'

'Maybe that's enough for her,' said Ollie, not quite believing it. 'Maybe all she wants is to cause as much death and destruction as she can.'

He noticed Jack frown, then turn once again to her computer.

'I know this is hard for you to speak about, Ollie, but . . . your parents. Tell me again what Sikes said to you. About her role in the terrorist attack, I mean.'

Ollie recounted what he remembered, his voice wavering as he spoke.

When he was finished he watched Jack with all the others. Somehow she was able to navigate from website to website faster than Ollie could follow. He saw her bring up news stories about the bomb on the bus that had killed his parents, wincing when he saw the photographs that had been plastered over the newspapers at the time. Mercifully, however, Jack quickly moved on to other things, and soon her computer screen was filled with graphs. Next, Maddy Sikes appeared in news coverage she'd generated herself: thick columns of text that seemed to have been drawn from the business sections of various websites.

'An experiment,' Jack said, all the while tapping keywords into her computer. 'Right, Ollie? That's what you said Sikes called it?'

Ollie rolled his lips and nodded his head. That word – so cold, so clinical – was almost the hardest thing for him to hear. His mum and dad had been killed – murdered – purely to satisfy Sikes's curiosity. And Ollie didn't even know about *what*.

'She was speculating,' Jack announced, leaning back from her computer.

'Specu*what*?' said Sol.

Jack swivelled her wheelchair to face them. 'Speculating,' she repeated. 'It means . . . betting. In a financial sense. Basically, the bomb that killed Ollie's parents is how Sikes made a whole ton of money.'

'How so?' said Dodge.

'A bomb goes off in a major city, and the first thing that happens is people panic. On the streets, but also businesspeople, investors, even governments. So stock markets crash, property prices plummet, meaning everything that was once expensive becomes cheap.'

'Because no one wants to buy it,' said Sol. 'Right? Like, who'd want to buy a skyscraper in London if people think it's going to get blown up the next day by a bunch of terrorists?'

He meant the question rhetorically, but Ollie gave him an answer.

'Maddy Sikes,' he said. 'Maddy Sikes bought everything she could, because she knew it wasn't terrorists. Because she was *ready*.'

'Exactly,' said Jack. 'So after that bomb, Maddy Sikes started buying when everyone else was selling. That's how she built her empire. She was making money before then, mainly from the smuggling Dodge mentioned earlier, but faking a terrorist attack . . . that's what took her to the big time. And with money, of course, comes power.'

'And now she's doing it again,' said Sol. 'But bigger, this time. Better.'

The others looked at him.

'Not *better* better,' Sol amended. 'Just . . . you know what I mean.'

'And that's why she's using Dr Gruber,' said Dodge. 'You talked about her ruling over a pile of rubble, Lily, but chemical weapons cause death, not destruction. It's not London Sikes is planning to destroy, because when the dust settles she wants to *own* it.'

'Right,' said Ollie, bitterly. 'It's just the people who live here she wants to murder. More trophies to add to her collection.'

All Ollie could see at that moment were the faces of his parents. Of Nancy. Of the people he'd loved who Maddy Sikes had killed.

'So let's *do* something about it, people,' said Flea. 'Let's not stand around moping.'

Ollie turned, and saw Flea had been looking directly at him.

'What, though?' said Lily. 'What *can* we do?'

'Should we go to the police?' said Sol.

Both Keya and Imani scoffed.

'And tell them what?' said Jack. 'Where's our evidence? Of *anything*?'

'And anyway, it would take too long,' said Dodge. 'By the time we got them to believe us – *if* we got them to believe us – it would be too late. No,' he announced, standing taller. 'We handle this ourselves. Keya, Imani, Ollie, you're the only ones who saw those ambulances. Was there anything – anything at all – that would help us locate them?'

Keya and Imani looked at each other helplessly. Ollie was so busy fuming at what Flea had said, he almost didn't hear Dodge's question.

'They all had the same number plate.'

As one the children turned. It was Harvey Hunter who'd spoken. The others had drifted towards Jack's computer, but Harvey was still seated at the map table. Ollie had completely forgotten he was there.

And he looked ill, Ollie saw. Paler, more terrified, than any of them.

'They all had the same number plate,' Harvey repeated. 'Those ambulances. They looked like clones, I remember thinking. Although I didn't figure it was important at the time.'

Of course, Ollie thought to himself. Hadn't he noticed something odd about the ambulances himself?

'But why would they all have the same plate?' said Lily.

'Because they were fakes,' Keya answered. 'Clones, like Harvey said. Sikes would have wanted them to be untraceable.'

'LD56 . . .' Harvey was reciting, eyes pinched as he tried to recall, but his voice trailed off. 'That's all I remember. Sorry.' He looked ashamed all of a sudden, perhaps as much for his behaviour earlier as for his failure to recall the number plate in full.

Dodge had crossed the room towards him. He laid a hand on Harvey's shoulder. 'It's a start, Harvey. Thank you. And who knows? Maybe it will be enough.'

'So we find the ambulances,' said Flea, summing up. 'And when we do we find the bombs. Right? So what are we waiting for? Let's get going!'

'Wait,' said Ollie. 'There's something else.' He glared at Flea, who narrowed his eyes in response. Did he know what was coming, Ollie wondered?

'Maddy Sikes had a map,' Ollie said. 'In her office. It had the gang areas highlighted, but that wasn't all. The Haven was marked on it, too. That's how I found our way back here.'

'But . . . that's impossible,' said Sol. 'How could Maddy Sikes know where the Haven is? How could *anyone*?'

'That's just what I was wondering,' answered Ollie, his eyes never leaving Flea's. 'And when me, Dodge, and Keya went back to the warehouse,' he went on, 'Maddy Sikes was expecting us. She knew we were coming.'

'What are you saying, PJ?' growled Flea.

'I'm saying we walked into a trap,' Ollie shot back at him. 'I'm saying *someone* told her to expect us. Someone standing in this room.'

Immediately there were howls of outrage.

'No way!'

'You've got it wrong, Ollie!'

'Do you realise what it is you're saying?'

Only Ollie stayed silent. Ollie . . . and Flea. Such was the uproar, they almost missed the clamour that was building in the corridor.

'QUIET!'

It was Dodge who commanded the silence, and when he did they heard it immediately. The thunder of feet, the frightened yells, and then, in the distance, the unmistakeable sound of a scream.

The investigations team started moving in unison. Lily reached the door first, and threw it open the moment her fingers touched the handle.

It took Ollie a panicked heartbeat to work out what he was seeing. There was smoke everywhere, and children were dashing across the central hallway in every direction, scattering like marbles. And when Ollie looked up, he saw what had caused them all to run. The Haven, above them, was on fire.

24 MADDY'S REVENGE

'We're under attack!'

Dodge grabbed hold of the boy who'd been running by. He'd been plunging down the central staircase, which was just along from the control room.

'Samir? What are you talking about? What's going on?'

'We're under attack!' the boy repeated. 'There are men . . . on the roof. They had bottles. With rags in the top. They lit them and threw them, and then the fire, it . . .' The boy was terrified, Ollie saw. The only colour in his skin was from the panicked flush to his cheeks and the smears of soot that dappled his hands and neck. He must have been right beside the fire when it broke out.

'*Go*,' Dodge told him. 'Head downstairs and get to safety. You know the drill. You've practised it a thousand times.'

There were screams, and Ollie and the rest of the team turned to look. More children were fleeing the floors above, and Ollie recognised some of the younger girls and boys he'd seen in Aunt Fay's garden. Behind them, being guided in her descent by two slightly older children, was Aunt Fay herself.

Ollie and the others dashed over to help. They caught up with Aunt Fay midway down the flight of stairs leading from the second floor, just as one of the girls helping Aunt Fay slipped. Sol caught the girl just in time. Ollie took her place at Aunt Fay's side, steadying the old woman.

'Ollie,' she gasped. 'Thank you. But you should go, all of you. I can manage the stairs if I take my time. To think, when I was younger I used to slide down the bannisters.' Aunt Fay gave a feeble smile. In her way, Ollie suspected, she was as terrified as Samir was. As they all were.

'We're not leaving you,' said Ollie.

'We're not leaving *anyone*,' agreed Dodge. 'Aunt Fay, are there any more children upstairs?'

'I don't think so. I called out, and no one answered, but it was all so confusing. What's happening, Dodge? Who are these people? And why are they attacking the Haven? Don't they know we try to *help* people?'

'It's Maddy Sikes,' said Flea to the entire group. 'It's got to be. She's taking her revenge for PJ and the other kids escaping.'

Somehow Flea made it sound like it was Ollie's fault. Like he'd acted selfishly by trying to save the children's lives.

'It's her revenge all right,' said Dodge, 'but I doubt it's Sikes's people. You said she knew where the Haven was, Ollie. All she had to do was put the word out that we were responsible for the missing kids, and any one of those gangs would have been happy to come after *us*.'

Ollie could feel the heat of the fire now, and the air was dense with smoke. The entire upper level was ablaze, he saw. If the fire had been set on the ground floor, the Haven might already have been lost.

There was the sound of smashing glass beside them, and as one the children leapt back. A bottle landed beside them, the flames from its burning wick spilling like water across the floor. The bottle must have been filled with something flammable. Petrol, Ollie guessed.

They looked up, and saw a man peering down at them from across the balcony. He had tattoos all along his forearms and a scarf wrapped across his face. As they stared up at him the man turned and fled. There were others up there, too, Ollie saw. Their mission accomplished, they appeared to be following the first man towards their escape route across the roofs.

'They're Diamonds,' said Imani. 'I'd recognise those tattoos anywhere.'

'I say we go up there and teach them a lesson!' said Flea. He started back up the staircase, but Dodge hauled him back.

'That's not going to solve anything. And anyway, how are you going to get up there?'

The way upstairs was blocked. As well as the flames that were devouring the third-floor mezzanine, a pile of rubble from the collapsing ceiling had filled the top flight of stairs.

'Look!' Keya was pointing where the Diamonds had been. A girl of maybe eight or nine was looking down. Once again Ollie recognised her from Aunt Fay's garden.

'Aunt Fay! Help me!'

'Mia!' Aunt Fay responded, the horror in her voice heart-wrenching to hear.

The girl was trapped, Ollie saw. Cut off from them the same way they were cut off from her.

Dodge didn't even hesitate. 'Lily, Ollie: follow me,' he said. 'The rest of you: double check the first floor, and then *get downstairs*. Flea, you're going to have to help Jack.'

A *crack* in the timbers above them was like the firing of a starting gun. Dodge was off, racing up towards the stranded girl, with Lily a short step behind him.

Ollie was still supporting Aunt Fay. He glanced at her uncertainly.

'Go,' she said, releasing her hand where she'd been clutching Ollie. 'But be careful,' she called as Ollie spun. 'All of you!'

Getting to the second floor was easy. There were just a few fallen bits of debris to avoid, and if it hadn't been for Ollie's wounded leg he would have been up the staircase in a handful of bounds. He caught up with Dodge and Lily at the barricade of fallen wreckage midway up the final flight of stairs.

Mia, above them, gave a shriek. She'd spotted Ollie and the

others heading towards her, and had moved to try to meet them halfway. But fire was raining down on her from the ceiling, and she seemed unsure where she should step. Ollie recalled the state of the floor on the uppermost mezzanine even before the fire had broken out, how it had resembled a patchwork of holes.

'Hold still, Mia!' Dodge called. 'We're coming!'

Ollie pulled his jumper over his mouth to try to filter out some of the smoke. Dodge and Lily did the same. They exchanged glances, and Ollie read the hopelessness in their eyes.

Dodge turned towards the wreckage and started to climb.

'Wait!' said Lily. 'Let me go. I'm lighter.'

Dodge hesitated, one foot already planted on the pile of rubble. As if to prove Lily's point, the piece of wood he was standing on collapsed from under him. It crumbled into dust like a piece of charcoal.

Lily forced Dodge out of her way. She checked the debris for a decent foothold, and then committed her weight. There was a snapping sound, and something shifted, yet whatever Lily was standing on held firm. But she was only a single step closer to Mia. She had another twenty to go at least.

'Help!' Mia shouted. 'Please! Help me!'

'Stay away from those bannisters, Mia!' Ollie called. In her fear of the encroaching flames, the girl had edged close to the handrail, and Ollie recalled how loosely it had been fastened.

The girl seemed not to hear him. She reached a hand to clasp the rail, and didn't appear to notice how far it tilted into the void. Ollie could tell it wouldn't hold out much longer.

Dodge saw it, too. 'Faster, Lily!'

Lily had the sense not to look back. She was glancing periodically at Mia, but her attention was mainly on where she was climbing. She was moving as rapidly as she could across the pile of debris, but almost at every step something below pulled greedily at her leg, threatening to draw her deep into the pile.

Somehow she made it to the other side. Only then did she allow herself the briefest glance behind her, and Ollie saw the sweat on her brow. Her smile was as much a tremble, and it only showed for an instant before she turned and started back towards the girl.

Mia was sobbing, staring down at the gaps beneath her feet. Ollie could barely tear his eyes from that bannister. At every snap, crackle and pop of the fire, he expected to see it break apart.

'Mia,' Lily was calling. 'Mia! Look at me, Mia!'

Lily was barely an extended arm's length away now, but she appeared to be as close to Mia as she could get. Ollie couldn't see the floor at Lily's feet, but from the way Lily was glancing nervously downwards, he imagined her teetering at the edge of a gaping hole.

Mia looked up then, and with a recklessness that revealed her panic, she flung herself blindly into Lily's arms. Lily caught her, but only just, and as Mia thrust herself away from the bannister, the handrail splintered and finally broke away. Ollie watched it tumble through the air, spinning and twisting almost gracefully before it fractured into a thousand pieces in the entrance hall below. It landed with a crash, missing the children fleeing the classrooms, but setting off another flurry of screams.

Ollie and Dodge shared a look that was mainly horror.

'Dodge! Ollie! Lily! *Hurry!*'

Ollie looked below him, and saw Sol was the only one still standing outside the control room. He was pointing towards the ceiling above Ollie's head. A huge oak beam had broken its mooring, and was in danger of swinging down right on top of them. It looked like a half-felled tree, and no doubt weighed just as much.

'Reach for us, Mia!' Dodge was calling. 'Hold out your hands!'

He and Ollie were as far up the pile of debris as they dared to climb. Lily was helping Mia up from the opposite side.

The girl slipped, screamed, but Lily stopped her from falling. Desperately, realising Mia wasn't going to make it on her own, Lily took hold of the girl around her waist and half threw her towards Dodge's and Ollie's extended arms. From the exertion showing on Lily's face, it clearly took every last ounce of effort she had.

But it worked. Ollie felt his hand closing around Mia's wrist, and Dodge grabbed hold of her from the other side. They hauled her over the mound of debris, ignoring the girl's cry of pain, and then they had her – she half jumped, half fell towards them, and Dodge scooped her from the rubble.

'Dodge, look out!' Ollie pointed, just in time.

Dodge spotted the falling chunk of plaster and, with Mia in his arms, leapt to one side before it hit. Mia had her hands locked around Dodge's neck. She was clinging to him so tightly, Ollie was surprised Dodge was able to breathe.

'Get her to safety!' Ollie told him. 'I'll stay and help Lily!'

With a pained glance towards his girlfriend, who was already halfway across the mound of wreckage, Dodge gave a single nod. And then he was off, darting between the falling wisps of fire as he carried Mia towards safety.

'Ollie? Help me, Ollie. I'm stuck.'

'I'm coming, Lily. Hold still!'

Ollie climbed again, but the mound was becoming more unstable. Twice his foot slipped, and when he flailed to try to catch Lily's hand, he swiped only thin air.

But then his trainer found purchase, and he was able to hoist himself up. Lily had almost made it to the crest of the debris herself, and this time when Ollie reached for her, he knew he'd be able to grab hold.

'I'm here, Lily. I've got—'

Ollie caught the movement in the corner of his eye. That beam Sol had spotted had broken free, and it was slicing through the air towards them like a scythe.

'LILY!'

The beam hit the mezzanine on Lily's side of the pile. It missed her legs, but smashed through the weakened floorboards. The effect on the mound of debris was instantaneous. There was just time for Ollie to meet Lily's eye before the hole behind her sucked her in and swallowed her up.

25 DEVIL'S PACT

'*No!*'

Ollie wasn't sure if it was him who yelled, or someone looking up from below. Sol, watching so helplessly from the first-floor mezzanine, or Dodge with Mia somewhere on the stairs.

But he didn't stop to consider. He threw himself forwards, towards the spot where Lily had been standing. The rubble beneath him began to slide into the fissure in the floorboards, slipping easily through the cavity like sand running through a timer.

Ollie allowed himself to be carried on the tide of debris until he was half hanging through the hole himself. Then he flung out an arm, bracing himself against the jagged opening that had been created by the fallen beam, and found himself staring straight into a ten-metre drop.

'Lily!' he called, scanning the wreckage beneath him. But there was no sign of her. Either she'd fallen to the floor below and been buried by the rubble completely, or . . .

'Ollie!'

Ollie twisted to the sound of the voice.

'*Lily!*'

Despite the situation, Ollie couldn't help but grin his relief. She was alive! Amid the rubble was a thick coil of cable, and Lily had found herself ensnared. The cable was twisted around her ankle, and she was clinging to the fallen beam with every last fingernail. If the beam slipped further, or the cable snapped, there would be nothing to save her.

'Take my hand, Lily! Quickly!' Ollie shuffled sideways, conscious the ground was shifting beneath him, and extended every tendon in his arm. His fingertips grazed Lily's as she released one arm from the beam, but her momentum swung her away from him like a pendulum. She tried again, missed again, and Ollie knew there was only one thing for it.

'Jump, Lily! You're going to have to jump!'

Lily, terrified, shook her head.

'I'll catch you, Lily,' Ollie told her. '*I promise.*'

Lily looked down, then back at Ollie, seemingly trying to decide how much she could trust him. She gave a nod.

'You're going to have to free your foot,' Ollie instructed. 'Unhook that cable, otherwise you'll get dragged back down again.'

It wasn't easy, but Lily managed to do as Ollie said. She tried shaking her foot loose, but in the end had to use one of her hands. For those several seconds, as Lily dangled one-handed above the abyss, Ollie could barely bring himself to watch.

'Ready?' said Ollie, when her leg was free. 'One, two, three . . . *jump!*'

Lily jumped.

The gap between them was only a couple of metres, but for one dreadful moment Ollie was convinced it was too far. Rather than flinging herself closer, Lily seemed to be falling away from him. But then her hands closed around his wrists, and Ollie's fingers locked around hers. He had her. Only just, but he had her.

And then he started slipping. It was the added weight. Without meaning to, Lily was pulling on him like an anchor.

'Ollie? What's happening, Ollie? We're falling!'

It was as though they were balanced on a pile of ball bearings, and once one had started to roll, all the others had begun moving as well. The slithering pile gathered momentum, and pieces of rubble started toppling through the hole. With his hands locked around Lily's, there was nothing Ollie could do. Not unless he let Lily go.

But he had no intention of doing that. If she was going to die, he was, too. Ollie's only regret, as he faced the reality of his impending end, was that they hadn't managed to stop Maddy Sikes.

'*Got you.*'

Ollie hadn't realised he'd shut his eyes. When he opened them he saw Lily's face grinning up at him. Grinning *past* him, in fact, at whoever had seized Ollie around his ankles.

'Sol!'

'Jeez, Ollie,' said Sol as he pulled. 'And I thought Flea was heavy.'

'It's not me,' Ollie answered, wincing as the rubble scraped his stomach. 'It's Lily. Big bones must run in the family.'

Sol spluttered. 'I'm warning you, mate, don't make me laugh!' He screwed his eyes, bracing his feet and arching his back.

'And I'm warning both of you,' came Lily's voice from down below. 'Call me big-boned again, and you'll end up wishing you'd let me fall.'

She let out a scream as Sol lost his footing. They only dropped a few centimetres, but to Ollie it felt like several metres. His stomach was somewhere near his mouth.

'Less talking,' Sol gasped. 'More *climbing*.'

With a final heave, he hauled first Ollie then Lily through the hole. Ollie never thought he'd be so grateful to find himself on the top floor of a burning building. He grinned at Sol, and Sol, breathless, beamed back.

But there was no time to celebrate. The fire was intensifying, the cackling wall of flames on the verge of cutting them off. If they didn't get down the stairs quickly, they would have no choice but to try their luck jumping after all.

'*Run*,' Sol said. He shoved Ollie forwards and grabbed Lily's hand, helping her as she struggled to her feet.

Halfway down the stairs they saw Dodge hurrying towards them from the opposite direction. He must have carried Mia to safety, and was coming back now to try to help.

When he reached them he flew straight into Lily, throwing his arms around her and practically knocking her to the floor. Lily gasped, then hugged Dodge back just as fiercely.

'I thought I'd lost you,' Dodge was saying – pleading, almost – into Lily's ear. 'I thought you were going to fall for sure!'

Lily scrunched her eyes and grinned. 'You don't get rid of me that easily,' she said.

'Um . . . guys?' said Sol, clearing his throat. 'I hate to interrupt, but the building? It's kind of on fire.'

Dodge and Lily broke apart. 'Right,' said Dodge. He quickly scanned the area around them. 'This way. Follow me.'

He led them down into the entrance hall, where the flood of children from the classrooms had barely lessened. But what Ollie had mistaken for panic from up above was just the opposite. The older kids had formed rescue teams, and were methodically sweeping the corridors to make sure none of the younger children were left behind. The figures Ollie had seen dashing back and forth were all part of a well-drilled evacuation plan being put into action.

'Oh, thank heavens!' said Aunt Fay, as the investigations team was reunited. She and the others were waiting for them under the shelter of one of the vast stone archways that circled the Haven's entrance hall. From their vantage point, they would have seen everything that had transpired on the floors above.

'Thank heavens you're safe,' said Aunt Fay again. She reached for Lily and pulled her close, before yielding her to her brother. Flea held Lily at arm's length, furiously checking her for signs of harm.

'Are you hurt?' he demanded. 'Did you get burnt? What on earth were you *thinking*?'

'I'm glad you're safe, too, little brother,' Lily answered, then took Flea by surprise by wrapping him in her arms. Flea stood startled, then relented and hugged her back. He met Ollie's eye over his sister's shoulder.

'There's no time to lose,' said Dodge. 'Song, you take Harvey and rescue Erik, exactly as we discussed. You're going to have to do it by yourself now. There's no time to round up that group of brown belts. Don't stop for *anything*, do you hear?'

Song nodded back at him, her expression all dour determination.

'I'll make sure she gets there safely,' said Harvey from the rear of the group. 'And I'll get your friend back home to you as well. Sorry about . . . everything,' he added. 'You lot are all right.'

Dodge nodded his appreciation. Ollie felt bad for having judged Harvey so harshly.

'Keya,' Dodge was saying, 'Imani: you two find the kids who were in the infirmary. You've got to get them back to their home turf. Let their gang leaders know they're safe and that Sikes was behind this whole thing. We need to *end this war*, and we'll need the gangs' help searching for those ambulances.'

'Sol and I will go with them,' said Jack. 'Tell the gangs what they're looking for.'

Dodge signalled his approval. 'Listen though,' he warned Jack and Sol. 'If you find those ambulances—'

'*When* we find them,' Sol amended.

Dodge smiled. '*When* you find them, don't go near them. Get everybody out of the area and call in the police. I know you probably *could* disarm one of those bombs, Jack, but you can't disarm twenty-two of them. We're going to need help with this. And when the police see those bombs for themselves, they're going to *have* to believe us about what Sikes is up to.'

Jack nodded her agreement.

'The rest of you,' Dodge went on, 'stay here and oversee the evacuation. Again, we've practised this a thousand times, so everyone knows what to do. When I get back, I'll catch up with you at the—'

'Wait,' interrupted Lily. 'What do you mean, *when you get back*? Where are you going?'

Dodge's jaw clamped tight. His stony gaze fixed on the fire raging behind him.

'I'm going after Sikes and that detonator,' he declared, and turned back as though daring anyone to challenge him.

'Fine,' said Lily. 'Me, too.'

'What? No,' said Dodge, 'it's too dang—'

'And me,' said Flea, cracking his knuckles.

'I'm coming, too.'

Dodge, Lily and Flea looked at Ollie.

'Sikes killed Nancy,' Ollie said. 'She murdered my parents. There's no way you're going after her without me.' *Plus*, he was thinking, *I'm not letting Flea out of my sight. Not after everything that's been happening.*

'But . . . your leg, Ollie,' Lily said. 'You can barely walk.'

'I'll crawl if I have to,' Ollie replied, more sharply than he'd intended, and he noticed Flea, in response, give a smirk.

'Ollie?' said a voice, concernedly. Aunt Fay had made her way to Ollie's side. 'All of you,' she amended. 'Remember, children, justice is one thing. Revenge is something else entirely. It's a pact with the devil. A prize that rarely comes without cost. Believe me,' she said, this time appearing to look directly at Ollie, 'I know.'

Ollie saw the fire reflected back at him in Aunt Fay's eyes. In their sheen he watched everything that Aunt Fay had dedicated her life to steadily being transformed into smoke and ash.

'I know,' she said again. 'I *know*.'

26 SMOKE LINES

Ollie's leg throbbed with every stride he took, but he'd meant what he said to Lily. There was no way he was letting the others go without him.

According to Jack, Sikes's plan to catch a private plane meant she would almost certainly be taking off from City Airport. Dodge had asked Jack how she could be so sure, and Jack's response had been categorical. *Because Sikes owns it*, she'd said. So that was where Ollie, Dodge, Lily and Flea were heading. They had to hope they'd worked out the timing of Sikes's plan correctly, and that she hadn't already taken off.

They had to hope as well that the others would succeed in their own missions without them. There was Song, who was running out of time to rescue Erik. There was Aunt Fay and the children in the Haven itself. Ollie was confident they'd get to safety, but what he didn't know was where they would go after that. Where *could* they go?

As for the rest of them, Jack, Sol, Keya and Imani had perhaps the toughest task of all. If Ollie and the others didn't manage to get hold of that detonator, dealing with the bombs would be down to them. And if they were to find them in the first place, they would also have to convince the gangs to work together, when they were currently busy tearing the city apart.

'This way, Ollie.'

Ollie had turned left in the tunnel outside the kit room. Dodge and the others had gone right.

'But . . . isn't this the quickest way into the sewer?'

'It is,' Dodge confirmed. 'But today we're going a different way. If we walked all the way to Docklands, Sikes would be on a beach sipping a pina colada by the time we arrived.'

'So how do we get there any faster?'

'How does anyone get around London when they're in a hurry?' Dodge replied. 'We take the Tube.'

They dashed along the access tunnel, and soon enough were splashing through a slightly larger tunnel puddled with water.

It wasn't long before they reached a doorway in the slime-covered wall, which Dodge illuminated with his phone. Ollie had never recovered his own phone after it'd been taken from him by Sikes's men, meaning he was relying on the others to spotlight his way.

'Ready?' said Dodge, primed to pull at the door.

'Ready,' Lily echoed back. Flea just nodded at Dodge grimly.

'Wait,' said Ollie, mystified. 'Ready for what?'

Dodge wrenched the door open, and immediately the tunnel was filled with a booming *roar*. Flea and Lily braced themselves by leaning forwards, but Ollie was physically driven back. It was as though Dodge had opened the door on to a hurricane.

Ollie felt Dodge grip his upper arm, helping to hold him steady.

'Stand firm, Ollie!' Dodge shouted. 'It'll pass!'

Sure enough, almost as abruptly as the windstorm had started, it stopped, and the roar was replaced by a deafening silence. Ollie wasn't certain at first whether or not his ears still worked.

'Right,' said Dodge, and the sound of his voice was unexpectedly normal. 'Let's go. Quickly. At this time of day, we've got four minutes at best.'

He led the way through the doorway, and Ollie saw he'd stepped into a train tunnel. That roar had been a London Underground train thundering by.

Ollie was about to follow Dodge through, when Flea hauled him back by his trailing hood.

'Hey,' Ollie protested. His hand went up to his throat, where his jumper had half garrotted him.

Flea shoved past him, bumping Ollie with his backpack. Once he was over the threshold, he shone his phone at the floor inside the Tube tunnel. 'That rail you were about to step on? It carries a current of over four hundred volts. But if you need a little spark in your life then please –' he swept an arm inviting Ollie to step on the rail – 'be my guest.'

Feeling stupid, Ollie could only stare at the harmless-looking train track.

Lily squeezed past him more gently.

'Flea's just mad at you for what you said back in the control room,' she said consolingly. She made to walk after her brother, then pulled up short. 'But you have to realise,' she added, 'Flea would give his life for the Haven. We *all* would.'

She seemed caught for a moment between a smile and a frown. In the end she simply turned away, and started following the others down the middle of the train tracks.

Ollie had to run to catch up, which wasn't easy with the light from his friends' phones dancing away from him, and his new awareness about the danger that was flowing beside him along those rails.

'The next station is just around this bend,' said Dodge. 'We need to get there before the next train heads our way, and up on to the platform without anyone seeing us. It goes without saying, Ollie,' Dodge added, glancing at Ollie across his shoulder, 'we don't tend to come this way except in emergencies. The risk is just too great.'

As if to demonstrate Dodge's point, there was a quivering in the rails: the early warning sign of a train approaching behind them. Dodge had hoped for four minutes' grace. By Ollie's estimation, they would be lucky to be granted a full two.

'Just our luck that the trains are running to schedule,' Dodge grumbled. 'I mean, seriously. When is there *ever* a good service on the Northern line?'

He started to run. Flea was right behind him, followed by Lily. Ollie found himself losing ground, his wounded leg slowing him down.

The quivering in the rails was getting louder, and soon the tunnel behind him began filling with light. A whip snap of pain in his injured leg caused Ollie to stumble, and all at once he was tumbling to the floor. He crash-landed, skidding forwards across the sleepers, and when he looked he saw his outstretched hand had missed the electrified rail by centimetres.

'Ollie! Get up, Ollie!'

The others had reached the entrance to the Tube station. It wasn't much further ahead, but that train was closing as well.

Ollie sprang to his feet. He started sprinting as fast as he could, driven on by the rush of air building behind him. The noise of the train had already overtaken him, so that Ollie could see the others shouting at him, urging him on, but he couldn't hear a word they were saying.

Ollie stumbled again, this time somehow managing to keep upright. He was yelling himself now, his own cry drowned out by the train's deafening roar. Up ahead of him, Flea and Lily were on the platform, bending to peer into the tunnel. Dodge was waiting halfway between the track and the platform, one hand locked on to Flea's, the other extended for Ollie to catch.

The train wasn't slowing down, and Ollie had time to wonder whether the driver was asleep at the wheel. He wanted to turn, to see how close the train was at his heels, but he couldn't risk falling again. And anyway, he could *feel* how close it was. It was like a monster breathing down his neck.

Ollie leapt, and for a moment thought he'd done so too early. But Dodge swung himself towards him, catching his arm, and then Flea hauled them both on to the platform. They collapsed in a knotted heap.

One, two, three seconds later the train rushed past them, slowing now as it skirted the curved platform as though nothing untoward had happened. Ollie and the others could only watch as the doors of the train hissed open. Seeing them lying on the platform, one of the passengers tutted. A little kid seated beside his mum just laughed.

It felt odd to be sitting on the Tube. Ollie was thankful for the rest, but it was the first thing that had happened to him in the past forty-eight hours that felt remotely normal. For something that had once been so routine for him, it was strangely unsettling.

They changed trains at London Bridge, and were near the end of the line when the train they were riding screeched to a halt inside the tunnel. The driver's voice came over the PA, advising the passengers they would be stuck for a while. There was some kind of disturbance near Canning Town, the driver said.

'The war,' muttered Flea. 'It's still raging, then.'

Dodge nodded at him bleakly. He checked around the half empty train carriage, then got to his feet. 'Come on,' he said.

They moved through the train to the rear-most compartment, and to the emergency exit right at the back. Dodge pulled the release lever, and the door jolted ajar. The passengers seated nearest turned to look.

'Apologies, ladies and gents,' said Dodge. 'Hopefully you'll never find out how much of an emergency this is.'

They dropped from the train on to the tracks. They had to trot all the way back to the previous station, and this time a guard spotted them clambering on to the platform. But luckily there was a crowd of commuters that Ollie and the others managed to lose themselves within before he could give chase.

They made their way up to the entrance hall, and by sticking tight to passengers with tickets, were able to sneak through the barriers. Moments later they were out on the street. Ollie for one was looking forward to breathing the fresh air, but as it turned out he had no time to enjoy it. As soon as they stepped outside, they saw for themselves why their journey had been disrupted.

It was as though they'd emerged into the middle of a protest march. Except there were no banners, and Ollie couldn't tell which of the groups was shouting for what. There was a furious mob on one side of the street, directly opposite the Tube station, and another further down the road. In between them, doing their best to keep the two groups apart, was a thin blue line of police officers in riot gear. Whatever the groups were shouting at each other was lost to Ollie in the angry clash of words.

A bottle was thrown, and Ollie and the others ducked. The police officers started to push towards one of the mobs, but then a firework was thrown from the opposite side, and the police seemed uncertain for a moment which way to turn. It was chaos out here, just as Jack had said.

'Shouldn't we do something?' Lily said, as Dodge herded them down a side street. 'Shouldn't we try to tell them what's been happening?'

'Look at them,' Flea answered, jabbing a thumb across his shoulder and then hooking it beneath the strap of his backpack. 'They wouldn't listen.'

'We need to trust Jack and the others,' agreed Dodge. 'Our job is to stop Maddy Sikes.'

Their journey to the airport took over an hour in the end. By the time they got there it was already the afternoon. Ollie couldn't help worrying about Erik. Danny Hunter's deadline had passed, meaning Song had either got him to safety, or . . .

Ollie shook his head. He didn't want to think about the alternative.

The airport was sited just beyond the Isle of Dogs, in a crook of the River Thames. The runway ran alongside a strip of water, meaning they had no choice but to approach from the south. They couldn't go through the terminal. If they weren't stopped at ticketing, they'd be collared at security for sure. Their only option was to find a way through the fence.

'Jack said the private hangars are in the south-east corner,' Dodge reminded them. 'If Sikes is anywhere, that's where we'll find her.'

Sikes was there all right.

Sitting in a bay at the far end of the runway was a huge Gulfstream G650, the biggest, fastest, flashiest jet money could buy. Ollie knew – he had a picture of one set as the desktop wallpaper on his computer. And this one had a personalised tail number: G650*MS*.

'Seems as if she wasn't in a particular rush, after all,' said Flea. 'Her plane hasn't even finished refuelling.'

'She probably wanted to stay for the start of the show,' said Ollie bitterly.

'Lucky for us,' put in Dodge.

'So how do we get in?' said Lily, staring at the fence. It must have been ten metres high, and there were security cameras covering every approach.

Dodge pulled out his phone. 'First we deal with those security cameras,' he said, frowning as he tapped something on his screen. He saw Ollie looking. 'Another one of Jack's modifications,' Dodge explained. 'Something she installed just for me. Using this app she built, I can scramble CCTV pictures, at least for a while.'

'Teacher's pet,' said Flea. 'I still don't see why I don't get to have that on *my* phone.'

'Your memory's clogged up with games,' Dodge answered, pointing his phone at the nearest security camera. 'There,' he said, looking at his screen again. 'That should give us cover until we reach the other side. They'll send someone along to check what's happened, but with any luck we'll be gone by the time they get here.'

'But . . . that fence,' said Ollie. 'There's no way we'll be able to climb that.'

'Who said anything about climbing?' said Dodge. 'The fence we deal with the old-fashioned way. Flea?'

Flea dropped his backpack on to the floor. He reached inside, and proudly produced a pair of heavy-duty cable cutters.

'There are some things technology can't fix,' said Flea, snipping the air. Then he hesitated, looking worried. 'You won't tell Jack I said that, will you? Last time I got in her bad books, she confiscated my phone.'

'And we can't have you missing out on screen time,' said Lily. 'Can we, little brother?'

They scurried from their point of cover towards the fence, and Flea set to work with his cutters. Soon he'd sliced a flap in the metal mesh big enough for them to squeeze through.

'Remember,' said Dodge, when they were ready to go, 'we need to take Sikes by surprise. If she sees us coming, she'll set off those bombs without even blinking.' He looked west, towards central London and the smoke lines from the fires across the city. 'And if they blow,' he added, 'it'll be our friends who'll die first in the explosions.'

27 ALL ABOARD

'They've finished refuelling, Ms Sikes. The captain says they're ready when you are.'

Sikes sat reclined on the leather couch in her private departure lounge. She kept her eyes closed, merely lifting a finger to acknowledge Grimwig's announcement, and waited motionless as he retreated from the room.

There was no rush. Ideally Sikes would have liked to have stayed and watched the 'festivities', as she'd described them to Gruber, from her panoramic office window. But there was no sense taking even the slightest risk with her own well-being, not when she was so close to achieving what she'd set out to.

And besides, if she timed it just right, and assuming the pilot stuck to the flight plan, Sikes would see everything from the window of her private jet. The only thing missing would be the sound of the screams.

One slight regret Sikes had was that Dr Gruber wouldn't be there to witness things. It was rare to find someone who could appreciate death to the same degree she did. In another life, she and Gruber might have conversed on the subject for hours.

Gruber's interest would have veered towards the technical – the precise molecular malfunction his unique strain of sarin gas would cause in the human body, for example – whereas Sikes's passion was more for the aesthetics of death: how it looked, smelt, sounded, *felt*. Nevertheless, they would certainly have had an interesting conversation.

There was no chance of that now, of course, not since Grimwig had sent the man toppling from the viewing deck of Sikes's skyscraper. That was one death Gruber *wouldn't* fully appreciate.

Sensing Bullseye growing agitated beside her, Sikes opened her eyes. No rest for the wicked, wasn't that the saying?

She checked her watch, taking a moment as she always did to admire the exquisite cut of the priceless diamonds that adorned the strap, and rose expensively to her feet. She straightened the slight creases in her Prada two-piece, and checked she had everything she needed.

Sikes didn't carry her own luggage, of course. Other than her jewellery and her watch, Sikes had with her only her tablet and a lead for Bullseye. He didn't normally wear one, but he took exception to air travel, meaning a lead on occasions such as these was often necessary. Sikes had no doubt Bullseye knew a flight was imminent. Probably that was why he was so restless, fussing and fidgeting where he lay. His ears kept twitching, too. Most likely he could hear the plane, thought Sikes. If they'd finished refuelling, the engines would be warming up by now.

Oh, and there was one other thing Sikes had with her. A tacky-looking item, as it happened, which normally Sikes wouldn't have permitted within a metre of her. It was a mobile phone, the type nasty little children carried, or people too cheap to upgrade from whatever their service provider offered free of charge. It was all plastic and spongy buttons, in other words. The sort of device that might easily get mistaken for a toy.

Why Gruber couldn't have used something more stylish, Sikes would never know. It wasn't as though she'd restricted his budget.

Still, so long as it worked. That was the main thing, Sikes supposed. And she had no doubt whatsoever that it would. She was even tempted to key in the code Gruber had given her right now. Four buttons, like a pin number, and then 'send' . . . and twenty-two glorious explosions would flower simultaneously right across the city.

But no.

There was no sense rushing things. And whatever else Sikes was, she wasn't reckless. If she detonated those bombs before she was up in the air, the risk to her would be small, but not non-existent. Gruber had engineered his poison gas to disperse quickly once the first batch of lives had been claimed, but it would linger for a day or two at least. And there was a breeze today, steadily slipping eastwards across the city.

Plus of course there were the explosions themselves to consider. Again, the destruction would be limited, because there was no sense destroying the very city she intended to own, but the nearest of the twenty-two bombs had been parked a mere kilometre away from where Sikes was currently standing.

'Bullseye? Heel, Bullseye. *Heel*.'

Honestly, what on earth was the matter with this dog? As well as fidgeting, he was growling now, too.

Sikes attached the dog's lead – a specially commissioned chain of brushed platinum links – and half expected Bullseye to fuss even more. As it was he barely noticed, but instead kept his teeth bared at something he'd spotted outside the window.

A plane taking off, thought Sikes, which didn't bode well for how the mutt would react when he spotted the familiar sight of Sikes's Gulfstream.

She led Bullseye from the lounge and through the departure gate. Although to be fair it was more as though Bullseye led *her*. If Sikes didn't know better, she would have sworn Bullseye was trying to get *on* the plane rather than away from it. But of course that was ridiculous. Bullseye wasn't a coward, but there were two things in life he would reliably run away from: air travel and baths.

As they crossed from the gate towards the Gulfstream, Bullseye gave a lurch, growling and barking furiously. A pain jolted Sikes's shoulder, and that was the final straw.

'Grimwig!'

Her assistant was waiting for her at the end of the carpet that reached tongue-like down the steps from the door of the aeroplane.

'*Grimwig!*' called Sikes again, and when the man finally scurried across to her, she thrust Bullseye's lead into his hand. 'Take him for a walk before you bring him aboard. Maybe he needs . . . I don't know. To take care of business or something.'

Grimwig struggled to hold the dog still. He wrinkled his already disfigured nose.

'Yes, Ms Sikes,' he replied, in a tone that Sikes found less than satisfactory. She hadn't forgotten about the candidate she had in mind to replace him, and if Grimwig didn't buck up his ideas, her assistant might shortly find himself meeting the same fate as the belated doctor.

Sikes strode on, conscious of Grimwig struggling to drag Bullseye off behind her. She mounted the steps leading to the door at the front of her plane. *Where is the pilot?* Sikes wondered, annoyed at the darkening of her mood. The captain was supposed to greet her at the top of the steps, a Vodka Martini waiting on a tray. Maybe Grimwig wasn't the only employee who would soon need replacing . . .

At the top of the steps, Sikes turned, her irritation easing slightly as once again she surveyed the skyline of the city. *Her* city. She breathed in deeply, anticipating the sweet scent of death, and closed her eyes as she savoured the moment.

Her moment.

But it was a mistake. Sikes realised she shouldn't have let her guard down the instant she felt a hand seize her wrist. Before she could react, she was being tugged inside the plane, the only door slamming shut behind her. She fell, humiliatingly, and all at once there were shadows looming over her. Sikes looked up, furious, but when she saw the faces glaring down at her, it was all she could do not to smile.

Well, well, well, thought Sikes. *Ollie Turner*. And there she'd been thinking life couldn't feel any sweeter.

28 TWISTED VISION

Ollie didn't like the gleam he could see in Sikes's eyes. For half a moment he had the horrible feeling it was him and the others who had walked into a trap, not her.

Sikes had dropped what she'd been carrying when Dodge had hauled her into the aeroplane, and Ollie saw her gaze sweep the floor. Right in front of her was an expensive-looking tablet, but that didn't seem to be the thing Sikes was most concerned with.

Rather, there was an old-school mobile phone lying beneath the closest of the huge leather passenger seats, a bit like the phone Nancy had given Ollie when he'd started at St Jerome's.

Sikes started crawling, reaching for the phone, but Ollie got there first. When he held it aloft, that gleam he'd spotted in her eyes was immediately extinguished.

'Give me that,' said Sikes, still on her hands and knees.

Ollie looked at the phone. There was only one possible reason Sikes would be carrying a phone like this one. The transmitter. The device Sikes needed to set off those bombs. This was it. Ollie had it in his hands.

'It's over,' he said. He was talking as much to himself, but when he heard the words aloud, he spoke them again, this time looking squarely at Sikes. 'It's over, Sikes. You've lost.'

'Is that it?' said Lily. 'The detonator?' She was standing by the door, making sure she'd closed it securely. Flea was at the threshold to the cockpit. It had been Flea's job to deal with the pilot, who was unconscious on his chair beside the control panel. Dodge was standing next to Ollie, staring down at Maddy Sikes.

Slowly, straightening her outfit as she rose, Sikes got to her feet. The investigations team closed in on her, braced in case she should try something. But there was nothing she could do. Ollie was right. It was over.

A hammering on the door made them jump. Through the window Ollie could see Sikes's assistant, Grimwig, trying to marshal Sikes's guards. There had only been four outside the hangar, as far as Ollie and the others had been able to work out. They'd evaded them easily, because the guards' attention had been focused towards the terminal.

Ollie heard a dog bark, and realised that Sikes's warg was out there, too.

'They can't get in here,' he said to Lily. 'Right? Not now you've sealed the door?'

'Not by hammering on it, they can't,' Lily agreed. 'But I can't guarantee they haven't got something else up their sleeves. I'll

258

She looked across Ollie's shoulder. 'Kill him,' she instructed. 'Finish the job I paid you to do at the beginning.'

For an instant Ollie simply froze. He could only blink as he tried to process what Sikes had said. When he turned he did so slowly. It was as if a grip of ice on his neck was controlling his movements, steadily – pitilessly – pulling him round.

Instinctively his eyes went to Flea's, and right away he realised the truth. It had only ever been Flea who Ollie had suspected. It was Flea who all along had most resented Ollie's presence, and who'd questioned every decision the investigations team had made. He was a troublemaker, a loudmouth, a bully . . .

But no traitor.

Neither was his sister. Lily was looking back at them all from her seat beside the pilot, showing the same confusion in her expression that Ollie felt.

Because she had realised it, too.

Dodge, ablaze with shame, was holding a gun levelled at Ollie's heart.

'I'm sorry, Ollie.'

Dodge moved back against the wall of the cabin, creating distance between him and the others.

'Lily?' he said. 'Flea? I'm sorry. I *am*.'

'*You?*' Ollie uttered. '*You're* the traitor?'

Dodge reddened further at the word. Flea gave a roar, and started forwards, but froze when Dodge swung the gun on him.

'Don't,' Dodge said. 'Please don't.'

'Dodge?' Lily was saying. The plane was still moving forwards, an expanse of tarmac ahead of them, but in her shock Lily had abandoned the controls. 'What's happening, Dodge? What are you doing?'

'Sit back down, Lily. I'm doing what I have to do, that's all.'

'But . . . what are you talking about? Why have you got a . . . a *gun*? Where did you get it? And why are you pointing it at—'

'*Sit*,' Dodge hissed, and Lily, stunned, shrank back into her chair.

'What are you waiting for?' came Sikes's voice. Ollie had almost forgotten she was there. 'Kill them. Kill them all. And begin with *him*.' She raised a finger and directed it at Ollie. She started towards him, no doubt meaning to reclaim the detonator, but as soon as she took her first step Dodge turned the gun on her.

'Don't you move!' he said, his voice shaking. 'Don't you . . . don't do anything!'

Sikes didn't appear afraid. She only looked disappointed. 'I'm beginning to question my decision to put my faith in you,' she said, sourly. 'Maybe Grimwig isn't such a bad assistant after all.'

'*Assistant*,' echoed Flea, incredulous. He rounded on Dodge. 'That's what this is all about? You're auditioning to be Mad Maddy's *dog walker*?'

'I'm not auditioning for anything!' Dodge retorted. 'And I never signed up for *this*,' he told Sikes. 'Kidnapping kids. Planting bombs. It's . . . it's *terrorism*.' The word almost choked him.

'You're signed up to whatever I say you are!' Sikes shot back. 'You know who I am, what I do. You've always known. So don't try to act all innocent! You handed me Nancy Bedwin readily enough. One life, a hundred, a hundred thousand. Tell me, boy, what's the difference?'

Dodge's eyes flicked towards Ollie. 'What happened to Nancy . . . that was you, Sikes. I just delivered her to you, that's all. You provided the manpower. I only . . . organised things. I never meant for anyone to die!'

Sikes barked her amusement. Ollie meanwhile couldn't help but stare at Dodge, powerless to keep the horror from his face.

'You were there,' Ollie said. 'That night, when they came to our flat. That was *you* waiting on the stairs.' Ollie remembered a shorter man standing with his arms crossed, the man he'd presumed to be in charge. It wasn't a man at all. It was a boy. Ollie's *friend*.

Ollie felt anger propel him forwards.

'You killed her,' he said, his voice rising from a dangerous whisper. '*You* did! And all this time you've been trying to kill *me*!'

263

It all made a twisted kind of sense. It was Dodge who'd led them back to the warehouse, just as Dodge had been the only one to escape. And when Ollie had climbed the ladder, and Dodge had reached down to try to save him . . . his hand had latched around Ollie's wristband, ripping the tracking device from Ollie's arm.

And later, when Ollie had turned up at the Haven alive, that expression on Dodge's face wasn't surprise. It was *shock*.

'I *saved* you,' Dodge said. 'Don't you see, Ollie? Right at the beginning. Sikes's guards would have killed you if I hadn't taken you to the Haven. What did you think, that I just *ran into* you after they shot Nancy? I was there for a reason. For you, Ollie. To protect *you*. It's like I said, I never wanted anyone to die!'

'And since then?' Ollie countered. 'What about since then, Dodge? Sikes wasn't happy that you let me go, was she? So you've been trying to deliver me back to her. Even here, now, that's what you're doing. She told you to bring me and you did!' Ollie felt his head shake, partly in denial, mainly in disgust. 'And you were willing to sacrifice your friends,' Ollie pressed. 'Flea, Lily. Your *girlfriend*!'

'I tried to do this alone!' Dodge countered. 'You're the ones who insisted on coming with me!' He shot a glance at Lily, who was watching in an obvious state of shock.

'What about Keya?' said Ollie. 'Back in the warehouse? You told *her* to come. You *made* her. You betrayed her the way you betrayed me!'

'She should never have run off in the first place! I was only taking her back where she belonged!'

'She belongs with her friends. With her family,' said Ollie. 'Not in the clutches of some mad woman!'

Dodge screwed up his eyes and shook his head. The gun barrel jerked dangerously in his grip.

'Forget about Keya,' Dodge said. 'None of us even knows her. And you, Lily. You, Flea. It's your fault you're here, not mine. Why is everything always down to me? *What should we do, Dodge?*' he mimicked. '*Oh, Dodge, help us, save us,* lead *us.*'

Once again Dodge shook his head, angrily this time.

'I'm *trying* to lead,' he said. 'Don't you understand? This, all of this –' he waved the gun barrel towards Sikes – 'was about me trying to save the Haven. It was *dying*. Sikes, she's promised us money. To help us rebuild. To help us restore the Haven to what it was. Didn't you say, Flea? Weren't you always arguing that we should take more people in? Well, this is how we do it. By using the money Sikes gives us.'

Flea was looking at Dodge as though he were a total stranger.

'You told her where the Haven was,' said Lily. 'It was like Ollie said in the control room. You weren't *saving* the Haven, Dodge. You *killed* it.' There were tears streaming down Lily's cheeks.

'You don't understand,' Dodge responded. 'I knew you wouldn't and you don't! You're as bad as Aunt Fay, all of you. Too stuck in the past. Too *idealistic*.' He said the word as though it were something distasteful. 'Sometimes you *have* to make a pact with the devil,' he insisted. 'Sometimes it's the only way you get to survive.'

All of a sudden it wasn't anger Ollie felt. It was sorrow. For his friends, for the Haven, for Dodge. He'd known no one on the investigations team would ever intentionally harm the Haven, and in that respect he'd been right at least. For in Dodge's mind, he was only fulfilling the responsibility he'd never asked for. He'd made a choice, a sacrifice: his soul for the Haven's future.

Or so, at the time, he'd believed.

'No one's coming,' Ollie said, his voice low. 'Are they, Dodge? You didn't message Jack. You didn't call the police. It's just us, alone, with Sikes.'

He looked at Sikes and saw her smile. It was an echo of that gleam he'd spotted when they'd hauled her inside the aeroplane. She was enjoying this, Ollie realised. Relishing every bitter moment.

'We can still stop this,' said Dodge, not quite convincingly. 'We can still stop those bombs going off. That's why I came here. It's the *only* reason I came.'

He looked at Ollie, Flea and Lily in turn, as though begging them to believe him.

'So why are you standing there pointing a gun at us?' said Flea, voicing what every one of them was thinking.

Dodge had no answer. His finger adjusted itself around the trigger.

'Give me the detonator, Ollie. I promise, after you're gone, I won't let Sikes set off those bombs. I'll make *sure* she doesn't.'

Sikes, at this, had heard enough.

'Stop deluding yourself, you foolish boy. There's nothing you can do now to stop anything. Just shoot him, and then give the gun and the detonator to me.' She started forwards once more, and again Dodge pinned her with the gun.

'No!' he said. 'I won't let you murder thousands of people! I *won't*.'

'You'll do as I tell you to do!' Sikes's voice was full of fury, but when she spoke again it was softer. 'You can still save your precious Haven, you know,' she said beguilingly. 'Maybe not the building, but your friends, the children you took on a responsibility to protect. With the money I'll give you, you can start again. Rebuild the Haven, only *better*.'

Dodge's eyes flicked towards her uncertainly. Ollie could see that he wanted to believe her. That he *needed* to.

'And you're right,' Sikes went on. 'There's no need for this glorious city to suffer. I'll deactivate the bombs. Every last one of them. You have my word, boy. My bond.'

'You . . . you promise? You *swear*?'

'Cross my heart,' Sikes said. 'And hope to die.' She looked at Ollie, her sickly smile broadening into something fouler. 'Now shoot him. Shoot Ollie Turner.'

'Dodge, don't, please,' came Lily's voice. 'Don't listen to her. She's lying. She's lied to you from the beginning. It's not your fault – you were only trying to do what was right. *Please*, Dodge! Please don't do this!'

Ollie couldn't tell if Dodge heard her or not. All he could be sure of was that Dodge wasn't listening. He'd reached a decision. Really, he'd made his decision a long time ago.

He turned the gun towards Ollie, his hands shaking. Then he swallowed and the gun barrel went still.

'I'm sorry, Ollie,' Dodge said. 'I truly am. But this is just the way it has to be.'

And his finger pressed down on the trigger.

29 FATAL SHOT

Ollie heard the shot before he felt it, and he knew instinctively that was the wrong way round. If the bullet had hit him, he would have been dead before the sound of the shot had reached him.

When he raised his head he saw Lily had lunged from the cockpit, throwing herself at Dodge in his blind spot. She'd forced his gun arm high, so that the bullet had fired into the ceiling.

'Lily!'

Dodge was bigger than Lily, and stronger. She was clinging to his arm as ferociously as Sikes's warg had clung to Ollie's leg, but it would surely only be a matter of seconds before Dodge managed to shake her off.

He lashed out with a fist, hitting Lily in her stomach. She had both hands locked around Dodge's forearm, meaning she had no way of blocking his blows. Ollie and Flea hurried forwards to try to help her, but in the narrow confines of the jet it was hard to get close. Dodge and Lily were whirling around like headless dance partners, locked together in some frantic waltz.

Flea got nearest, but as Lily and Dodge spun, the butt of the gun arced full force into Flea's temple. He staggered, and collapsed across the arm of a nearby seat.

Ollie attempted to grab Dodge's shoulder. Such was the ferocity of Dodge and Lily's struggle, he found it impossible to get a grip. If he'd had both hands free it might have been easier, but there was no way he was letting go of the detonator. He was aware Sikes was right behind him, watching the phone as closely as Ollie and the others were watching the gun.

Lily gave a shout, like a war cry, and made a final, desperate effort to recover the revolver. She clawed at Dodge's fingers, ignoring the blow he landed in her kidneys, and for an instant Ollie thought Lily had succeeded. He saw the gun slip from Dodge's hand, and Lily's fingers close around the barrel. But then Dodge's free hand forced Lily backwards, and the gun was tumbling towards the floor.

Either as it landed or just before it fell, the revolver went off again. The barrel must have been pointed towards the cockpit, because the bullet missed the unconscious pilot by centimetres. It hit the control panel, and there was a detonation of glass and smoke.

Instantaneously the plane gave a lurch, veering from the tarmac towards the grass that bordered the main runway. Steadily it began picking up speed.

Worse, Ollie had dropped the detonator. When the bullet had hit the control panel and the plane had swerved, he'd been thrown to one side and the phone had spilled from his hand.

He looked around frantically, certain it couldn't have gone far. He saw Lily on the floor a couple of metres away, Dodge lying dazed on top of her and Flea still hinged across the seat. He saw the gun lying unclaimed in the middle of the aisle . . . but there was no sign of the mobile phone.

Sikes was beside him. When the plane had veered she'd fallen, too, and Ollie knew she was hunting for the same thing he was. It was just a question of who would spot it first.

Sikes started moving, wriggling along the aisle like some mutant snake. She even hissed as she drew level with Ollie, her desperation to recover the detonator a primal, animal instinct.

Ollie looked . . . and saw it, too. The phone was right next to Flea, tucked in the shadow of the leather seat. Flea was still recovering from the blow he'd received to the side of his head. Even if Ollie shouted, Sikes would get to the phone before him.

If Sikes was moving like a snake, Ollie sprang forwards like something feline. His foot landed on Sikes's hand and he felt the crunch of her fingers beneath his heel.

Sikes gave a shriek, whether in pain or frustration, Ollie couldn't tell.

And he didn't care. All that mattered was that he would reach the detonator first. He was past Sikes now, blocking her way. It didn't even matter that when Ollie landed, he knocked the phone further beneath the seat. All he had to do was reach under the footrest and the detonator would be safely back in his hands.

'Flea!' he yelled as he scrabbled. He'd caught sight through the cockpit window of where the jet was headed: directly into the path of a landing plane. 'The controls, Flea! You need to stop us going on the runway!' Ollie was on his hands and knees again, shoulder deep beneath the seat. '*Flea!*' he said again, and this time he saw Flea stir. He looked down at Ollie, and then around, and with barely a pause to work out what was happening, he was lurching off towards the cockpit.

Ollie continued hunting for the detonator, angling his head now to try to see. The phone had been right in front of him. He just had to be careful not to knock it any further forwards, because if he did he doubted his arms would be long enough to . . .

Got it.

Ollie didn't know if he'd ever felt such relief. All he had to do was pull the phone free and stamp on it, the way he should have done when he'd first picked it up. And then, no matter what happened to Ollie and his friends, Jack and the others would be safe. *London* would be safe, and Nancy's mission – the work she'd dedicated her life to – would be complete.

The gunshot, when it came, was shock enough, but the scream that followed it was like a knife to Ollie's gut.

He spun, looking for Lily, because it was her cry he'd heard, Ollie was certain. All he could think was that Dodge must have recovered the gun before she could, but surely there was no way he would have *shot* her. He loved her, didn't he? Not everything about Dodge could have been an act.

It was Lily who'd screamed all right. She was bent over beside Dodge, on top of him almost, and Dodge was sprawled in the aisle. He was clutching his stomach . . . though there was nothing he could do to stop the blood. It stained his T-shirt, his trousers, the floor beneath him, flowing steadily from the place he'd been shot.

Maddy Sikes was looking down at him triumphantly. She must have abandoned the detonator when she'd realised Ollie would get to it first and had picked up the gun instead.

'Such a waste,' Sikes said, mockingly, as though she didn't really believe it at all. 'But I'm afraid that's what happens to my employees when they outlive their usefulness.'

Dodge was looking at Ollie despairingly, mirroring the shock Ollie felt sure he was displaying himself. Dodge reached for him, and Ollie tried to go to his aid, but Sikes immediately swung the gun.

'Stay where you are! And you –' she turned the gun towards the cockpit, aiming this time at Flea – 'get control of this aeroplane. *Now!*'

'It . . . it doesn't work,' Flea stuttered. 'The controls . . . they're busted.'

The jet was still heading towards the runway. Even if they managed to avoid the plane that had started its approach, there were airport vehicles parked directly in their path. And one of them, Ollie thought, looked like a fuel tanker.

Out of nowhere there was a blast. For a moment Ollie thought he had imagined it, that he'd had a premonition of the explosion that was to come. But the others had heard it, too – Sikes included. It sounded like a distant firework. But a big one, like the showstopper at the end of a display.

The bombs. One of them had gone off. Meaning no matter what happened now, Ollie and the others were already too late.

But then Ollie remembered he had the detonator in his hand. There was no way one of the bombs would have gone off, not unless . . .

Ollie looked at Sikes, who was staring at her diamond-encrusted watch with a mixture of rage and confusion.

'They found them,' Ollie heard himself saying. 'Jack and the others, they found the ambulances!'

There was no way he could be certain, but Ollie felt sure of it in his gut. That blast they'd heard was a *controlled* explosion. The police had disarmed one of the bombs. At least one, in fact. They might already have deactivated others that were further away.

Sikes let out a shriek of pure fury. She whipped the gun barrel towards Ollie.

'Careful, Sikes,' Ollie said, and he held out the detonator in front of him. 'You wouldn't want to damage anything valuable.'

Sikes almost allowed herself to take the risk; Ollie saw it in the tension of her grip.

Instead she said, 'You're right,' and she directed the gun so it was pointing at Lily. 'GET BACK!' Sikes roared, when Flea moved to protect his sister. Lily was still crouched beside Dodge. She'd managed to get Dodge's arm around her shoulder, but he was bleeding profusely from his stomach. He was conscious, but even if they managed to get him out of this plane, Ollie doubted Dodge would live.

'Give me the detonator,' Sikes said. '*Now*, Ollie Turner. Every second you make me wait, I fire a bullet.'

'No!'

Sikes had made to squeeze the trigger. Ollie had no choice but to do as she said.

'Ollie, don't!' said Lily. 'Don't give it to her! She's going to kill us all anyway!'

Ollie knew that Lily was right. But if he *didn't* give Sikes the detonator, she would shoot them all regardless, and then recover the detonator herself. This way he would buy them precious seconds, though for what Ollie could not have said.

He moved from the seat towards the others, holding both hands above his head. He tried to think, to work out some way they might still win. But the jet was heading relentlessly towards the runway. In less than a minute they would collide with that fuel tanker, unless the plane that was descending landed on them first.

And Sikes was aware of it, too. She'd started backing towards one of the emergency exits, no doubt preparing herself to throw it open the moment Ollie handed her the phone. All the while she kept the gun levelled at Ollie's friends, ready to fire should one of them make a move.

It was hopeless.

Except . . .

Dodge. Sikes had given him up for dead, but Ollie could see the fight left in his eyes. And as Ollie drew closer to Sikes, Dodge signalled with the slightest of nods.

Ollie hesitated. He saw what Dodge intended to do, and he knew full well what it would mean. But when Sikes lunged to grab the detonator, the decision was taken from Ollie's hands.

Dodge threw himself forwards, surprising Lily as much as he did Sikes.

Sikes spun, but too late.

Dodge smothered her, the gun, too. But it went off, and Ollie saw just enough of Dodge's face as he fell forwards to catch the pain that flared in his eyes.

'The pilot, Flea!' Ollie yelled. 'Grab the pilot!'

Flea reacted as quickly as Ollie had hoped. He darted for the pilot, dragging him from his seat and towards the exit. Ollie grabbed hold of Lily's hand, hauling her up and yanking her towards the door. Lily pulled down hard on the emergency lever and the door immediately fired open. It flipped, somersaulting, and clattered across the rolling tarmac below. They'd reached the runway, Ollie realised, meaning they had seconds left at best.

'Dodge?' said Lily, turning. But even she could see Dodge was gone. His lifeless body lay sprawled on top of Sikes, pinning Mad Maddy to the floor.

'Jump, Lily!' Ollie yelled above the engine noise, which was all the louder in the sudden rush of air. 'You have to jump!'

That fuel tanker was looming through the cockpit window, steadily filling up the glass.

Lily took one last glance at Dodge, her face crumpling in dismay. Then she turned and jumped towards the tarmac. Ollie saw her roll when she hit the floor.

'Go!' Ollie yelled to Flea. Flea met Ollie's eye, just for a second, and then he tumbled through the doorway, clutching the pilot with him as he went. They landed in a graceless bundle, only narrowly avoiding the aeroplane's wheel.

'*Noooo!*'

Ollie was about to jump himself when a hand closed around his ankle. It was Sikes, flailing with her one free hand to try to thwart Ollie's escape. But it was her weak hand, the one Ollie had trodden on, and he had no trouble prising her fingers free. He had time to do one last thing before he leapt towards safety, the detonator firmly in his grip.

30 PARTING GIFT

The plane struck the refuelling lorry right in the centre of the tank, and the crunch of glass and metal was like the sound of a rubbish truck being swallowed by an earthquake. The leaking fuel ignited with a *whump*, almost like an afterthought. Within seconds the heat was astronomical.

Ollie lay sprawled on the tarmac. The fire was raging just behind him, meaning he'd had less time before the collision than he'd thought. He'd been lucky, he realised. Incredibly lucky. Although he didn't feel particularly lucky right now. Yes, Sikes was gone, but so was Dodge. Maybe this was what Aunt Fay had meant about revenge never coming without cost.

Ollie raised his head to try to locate his friends. They were further back along the runway than he'd expected. The plane must have been travelling faster than Ollie had realised. Lily was already on her way to Flea, who was kneeling beside the unconscious pilot. Ollie staggered to his feet and went over to join them.

On his way he found Sikes's mobile phone. The detonator, which must have tumbled clear when Ollie had fallen from the plane. It was in pieces. The antenna had snapped and the battery was hanging from its compartment. Ollie stamped on it, just to make sure, grinding the circuit boards beneath his trainer.

'Ollie,' said Lily, as he approached. 'My god, you look . . . Are you OK? How are you even standing?'

Ollie knelt beside Flea over the unconscious pilot. 'Is he alive?'

'He's alive,' Flea answered. 'He's barely even scratched.'

The same couldn't have been said for Lily or Flea. Only the pilot, it seemed, had escaped the fall without injury.

'Come on,' Ollie said. 'We need to get out of here.'

In the distance he'd spotted a group of people rushing towards them. He couldn't tell whether they were airport employees or Sikes's guards, but he had no intention of sticking around to find out.

'What about him?' Flea said, gesturing to the pilot.

Ollie looked down. 'He'll be fine. Who knows? Maybe when he wakes up he'll think it was all a dream.'

No one spoke on their journey back to the Haven. Public transport was suspended, so they had no choice but to make the trip by foot. All the way they were braced for the sound of explosions, for the screams of innocent passers-by. But none came.

Ollie knew what they would find when they got home, but even so the sight of the burnt-out building was another body blow.

The Haven was a husk. It was a ruin of a ruin, a once magnificent monument reduced to a blackened shell. For Ollie, the sight was bad enough. For Lily and Flea, it must have felt as if they were staring at a tomb. More than a home, the Haven had been their harbour: a place that had sheltered them from life's storms. And now it was gone. Ripped from their lives the way their friend had been. It was a victory that felt as much like a defeat.

Flea was the first to recover himself. 'This way,' he said, turning abruptly, clearly trying to hide the emotion on his face.

Lily was crying more openly. She stood staring at the building with tears rolling down her cheeks. She was sad for the Haven, Ollie knew, but he could tell she was mainly thinking about Dodge.

'Lily?' said Ollie softly. He took her hand.

Lily smiled at him, and allowed him to lead her off towards her brother. Flea was waiting in the gap between two fire engines, still doing his best not to show his face.

They had to duck beneath a cordon erected by the emergency services, but nobody was looking their way. Flea led them into the cemetery through which they'd entered the Haven last time, and stopped beside the same overgrown grave.

'Where are we going?' Ollie asked him.

'The life raft,' Flea said, and without any further explanation, started his descent into the tunnels. Lily went after him, leaving Ollie no choice but to follow.

Once below, they walked away from the Haven rather than towards it. They turned left, right, right again, until Ollie lost all sense of direction.

Eventually Flea stopped beside a wall at the end of a narrow offshoot from the main tunnel. It reminded Ollie of the door by which he'd first entered the Haven, the one with the hidden camera and the fingerprint scanner. It made Ollie think of Dodge, and the memory was like a punch to his heart.

Just as Dodge and Ollie had done back then, Flea pressed his finger to a spot on the wall. A secret door cracked open almost reluctantly, as though it wasn't accustomed to people passing through.

Flea stepped to one side. For the first time since the aeroplane, he allowed his eyes to meet Ollie's.

'After you,' he said.

Ollie thought he was past being surprised, but he couldn't help showing his astonishment. They were still underground, but in contrast to the dark and dankness of the sewer, they'd entered a hallway that was filled with light.

'Is this . . .' he started to ask, but Ollie knew exactly what it was. He'd read about places like this, and had even spotted one or two on his journeys along the Underground, though he'd had no idea any were in such a good state of repair. 'It's a ghost station,' he said. 'Right? An abandoned Underground station.'

Flea nodded. 'Dodge always called it our life raft,' he said. 'It was one of the things he always insisted on, that we keep this place kitted out just in case we ever needed it. There's electricity, running water and space enough for us all. It's not a long-term solution. No one wants to live underground. But at least we're spared from sleeping on the streets.'

'Erik!'

As Flea finished speaking, a group of children appeared at the far end of the hallway. Jack was there, and Song . . . and Erik.

Lily was already rushing forwards. Before Ollie could follow her, Flea seized hold of his elbow.

'Listen, PJ,' he said, angling himself so that none of the others would hear. 'Don't think I'm going to forget what you accused me of. And I saw the way you looked at me on that plane.' Flea was holding Ollie tightly, his meaty fingers squeezing Ollie's flesh. But then he released his grip, and held out his other hand for Ollie to shake. 'But you stopped Sikes. And you saved my sister. Meaning for the time being I reckon we can call it quits.'

Ollie accepted Flea's outstretched hand. They shook, once, and then turned to be reunited with their friends.

*   *   *

'Ollie!'

Jack was the first one to greet him. Then Song rushed over to give him a hug, and Ollie, Flea and Lily found themselves at the centre of a circle. It was as though the entire population of the Haven had turned out to greet them. Ollie spotted Aunt Fay towards the rear of the group. Somehow she seemed to know where Ollie was standing, and sent a smile his way.

So this was where Aunt Fay and the others had run to. *The life raft.* It was perhaps more apt a description of the place than Dodge had ever anticipated.

Dodge.

Ollie looked at the faces of his friends as they gathered around him, and realised Lily must already have told them what had happened. Their smiles were tinged with sorrow.

'Is everyone safe?' Lily was asking. 'Did everyone manage to escape the fire?'

'Everyone's safe,' Jack confirmed. 'Including Erik here, thanks to Song. She got to Danny Hunter just in time.'

Lily gave Erik another hug, before Erik untangled himself and faced Ollie.

'Thanks, Ollie,' Erik said to him. 'From what I hear it's because of you I'm still in one piece. Literally,' he added, to everyone who was listening. 'Danny Hunter had started taking bets on how many fingers of mine he could chop off before I fainted.'

'I'm . . . I'm glad you're safe, Erik,' Ollie told him. 'I'm just sorry you had to go through that.' He pumped Erik's hand, counting them both lucky that he was still able to do so.

There was hardly enough space in the hallway to accommodate all the children. On closer inspection Ollie realised it was in fact another tunnel, wider than most because of the stairs that had once existed at one end. The stairwells themselves had long been blocked off, cutting the space virtually in half, but it didn't matter. It felt good to be pressed together so tightly, Ollie thought. Somehow, after everything, it felt *right*.

'Where's Sol?' Ollie asked, glancing around. 'And Keya, Imani . . .'

'They're still out there,' Jack answered. 'But we've kept in contact. We know they're safe.'

'So the ambulances,' Ollie prompted. 'The bombs . . .'

'We found them,' said Jack. '*All* of them. Thanks to Keya, Imani and the rest of the kids you freed. The police took a little persuading, but as soon as Sol and I showed them a photograph of what was inside one of those ambulances, they moved faster than a five year old on Christmas morning.'

Ollie felt weak with relief. It *was* over. Now that he knew it for certain, and he was sure everyone was safe, he felt barely able to hold himself up.

'Whoa,' said Erik, steadying him. Song caught Ollie's weight on the opposite side.

285

'Let's get you three some attention,' said Jack, frowning at Lily, Flea and Ollie. 'You look like someone threw you from an aeroplane and forgot to hand out the parachutes.'

Ollie smiled weakly, unsure whether Jack got her own joke.

The children around them cleared a path, and Ollie, Flea and Lily were led from the hallway into an adjacent tunnel. This one was narrower, and lined on one side with bunks.

Erik helped Ollie on to a mattress and propped a pillow behind his head. He was saying something to Ollie about his injuries, about how he'd probably need an injection for his leg. Jack was there as well, looking at Ollie concernedly, but in the same way that Erik's voice began to fade, Jack's face seemed almost to be dissolving.

Knowing what was happening but unable to fight it, Ollie drifted into sleep.

'Ollie? Ollie. Wake up, Ollie.'

'Nancy?' Ollie groaned. He wriggled away from the hand that was rocking his shoulder.

'It's me, Ollie,' said the voice. 'It's Sol.'

'Sol?' Ollie forced open his eyes. 'Sol,' he repeated, offering his friend a groggy half smile. 'You're back,' Ollie said. 'You're safe.'

Sol grinned down at him. 'I am. Although to be honest, I don't feel as if I was ever in much danger. Not compared to you, anyway.'

Ollie ground his palms into his eyes. 'How long have I been asleep?'

Sol checked the watch on his wrist. 'Well, it's eight a.m. now, and I got back last night at around eleven. So nine hours at least.'

'Nine hours?' Ollie sat upright with a jerk. It was a mistake. His battered body wasn't ready for such sudden movements. '*Ow*,' Ollie uttered, voicing the sound on a long exhalation.

'Are you OK?' Sol asked him. 'What hurts?'

'Just . . .' But Ollie struggled to narrow it down. 'Everything,' he said in the end. And he didn't mean only physically. Now that he was fully awake, he found himself remembering everything that had happened. He looked at his friend. 'You heard about Dodge?'

Sol bobbed his head. 'I heard.'

'He was a hero, you know,' said Ollie. 'We wouldn't have got out if it hadn't been for him.'

Once again Sol nodded. 'Everyone's talking about it,' he said. 'They're talking about you, too, you know. About what you did.'

Ollie wondered what exactly Sol meant. As far as he was concerned, he'd barely done anything, other than fall badly from a moving plane.

'I've got a surprise for you,' Sol announced, attempting to lighten the mood. 'Here.' He thrust a cereal bar at Ollie.

'A Tracker?' Ollie said. 'You woke me up to give me a Tracker?'

'What?' said Sol, confused. 'Oh. Right. No. I mean, yes, but . . .' He shook his head. 'The Tracker's not the surprise. Come on, get your lazy bones out of bed and I'll show you. You can eat the Tracker as you walk. And you're welcome for that, by the way.'

Ollie slid reluctantly from beneath the covers. He was still dressed in the clothes he'd been wearing since . . . he wasn't sure exactly. All he knew was that at some point he could use a fresh T-shirt and maybe – hopefully – a shower.

Sol was leading him back towards the entrance hall. He gestured to the other Haven kids in their beds, and held a finger to his lips. Ollie saw Flea face down in his pillow, and Lily muttering darkly in her sleep. He would have liked to have roused her from her nightmare, but he knew that dreaming, in the end, would do her good. Ollie hadn't had any dreams last night himself, at least as far as he remembered, but he didn't doubt his nightmares were still to come.

Even so, Ollie felt better than he had in a long time. Not physically. Physically he was a wreck. It was mentally, rather, that he felt repaired. How he must have needed those nine hours of sleep.

They turned into the main hallway, and Ollie came abruptly to a halt. Grinning, Sol moved to one side.

Right in front of him, standing next to Aunt Fay, was Keya. And beside them, talking to Jack, was Imani. But that wasn't all. Behind them stood twenty or so other children, and Ollie recognised them all. They were the kids Maddy Sikes had kidnapped, the gang members Ollie had helped free.

One of the children spotted Ollie – the boy who'd sacrificed his watch – and Ollie was stunned to see him start to clap. Soon everyone in the hallway was applauding. Ollie showed his bafflement to Sol, whose only response was to offer Ollie a shrug.

'What's going on?' Ollie asked as he drifted into the middle.

Keya flummoxed him further by leaning forwards and kissing him on the cheek. 'They're grateful, Ollie. We all are. You saved them, which is how they managed to save their friends.'

'But . . .'

It was all Ollie could think to say. And then he saw something pinned to Keya's top. A little H, the middle line drawn longer than it should have been and the entire letter framed by a triangle.

'What's that?' Ollie asked her, pointing. 'Does that mean . . .'

'It means I'm staying,' Keya confirmed. 'We all are. Every one of us.'

Ollie looked more closely and saw the other children bore the Haven's mark, too. Jack had a box in her lap. It seemed she'd been handing out badges.

'That's where you've been?' Ollie said. 'This is what you've been doing?' He looked at Sol, Keya and Imani in turn.

'If we're going to rebuild,' said Jack, 'we're going to need some extra pairs of hands.'

'Rebuild?' Ollie echoed, looking at Aunt Fay now. 'But the Haven . . . it was destroyed. Surely we can't stay in the ghost station for ever. I figured we'd all eventually have to leave. To go back to . . . to . . .'

'Go back to what, Ollie?' said Aunt Fay. 'Most of the children here don't *have* anywhere to go. And the Haven isn't just a building, remember. It's an idea. An ideology. It takes more than a fire to destroy something as powerful as that.'

Ollie looked around at the crowd of faces. It was hard to be disappointed when confronted with such optimism. Ollie couldn't help regretting not spotting Harvey Hunter, but perhaps that would have been too much to hope for.

'Oh,' he said, patting himself down. 'I almost forgot. Maybe this will help as well. You know, with the rebuilding.'

He dipped his hand into his pocket. There were gasps as he showed the others what it contained.

'Isn't that . . .' Keya began.

'Maddy Sikes's watch,' Ollie finished. He'd yanked it from Sikes's wrist and thrust it deep into his pocket just before he'd thrown himself from the plane. Knowing how close he'd come to being swallowed in the explosion, in hindsight he should probably have let it go. But it had seemed worth it, given the reward. After the fire at the Haven, he'd felt sure it would be of use somehow.

'Here,' said Jack. Wide-eyed, she'd accepted the watch from Ollie, but she was offering him something in return. A badge, like the ones she'd handed out to all the others. It was the last one remaining in the box.

Ollie understood what it meant. 'But I'm not . . . I mean, I can't . . .'

'You said "we",' Jack answered, matter-of-factly.

'Sorry?'

'You said "we". When you were talking about rebuilding the Haven. Meaning you've already decided you're a part of this, too.'

'She's right, mate,' put in Sol, helpfully. 'You definitely said "we".'

Ollie felt a lump run down his throat. It was what he wanted, there was no question of that. And really, he didn't know why he was even hesitating. He'd long decided that the Haven was doing exactly the sort of job Nancy had. The type of job Ollie had always wanted to do, even though he'd never quite figured out in what capacity. Nancy, the kids at the Haven, Aunt Fay – they were all trying to make the world a better place.

What worried him was whether or not Nancy would have approved of Ollie staying. He'd been back and forth in his mind trying to work it out, but now . . . Maybe it was wishful thinking, but Ollie couldn't help but think she would have. She'd have told him to be careful, to stay out of danger, but she would have been proud of him, Ollie was sure. The way he was proud of *her*.

Ollie accepted the badge in his outstretched palm. He felt Aunt Fay lay a hand on his shoulder.

'Now that's settled,' said Jack, 'we're also going to need someone to lead us.'

'I . . . what?'

'The Haven's not going to lead itself, Ollie Turner.'

'No, I know, but *you* should do that. You're the obvious candidate.' Not counting Nancy or Aunt Fay, Jack was by far the smartest person Ollie had ever known.

Jack made a face, one that reminded Ollie of the first time he'd met her, when she almost ran her wheelchair across his toes. 'Being in charge would mean I'd have to *talk* to people,' she answered. 'And no one else would enjoy that any more than I would. Plus,' she added, 'when would I get time to play on my computers?'

'Then . . . Lily,' Ollie suggested. 'One of the others.'

'There's no way Lily would step into Dodge's shoes,' said Jack. 'As for the others . . . Erik wouldn't want the job if you offered it to him. The same with Sol. *He* wouldn't do it if you paid him. Right, Sol?'

'*Are* you offering to pay me?' Sol said. 'Because, you know, depending on the salary . . .'

'The salary's what it's always been. Plenty of danger and not enough sleep.'

'In which case, thanks but no thanks,' said Sol. 'I'm kind of partial to my Sunday morning lie-ins.'

'Flea then,' said Ollie. 'What about Flea?'

He caught Jack and Sol share a look. 'Flea . . . might be a problem. He'll put up a fight, that's for sure. After Dodge, he always considered himself the next in line. But after what happened with Dodge, I think we all agree we need someone more . . . democratic.'

Ollie cast around at the faces before him. He was aware that most of the other Haven children were present now, too, having been roused from their beds by the sound of clapping.

'But why me?' he said. 'What makes me any better qualified than anyone else? Keya, say. Or Imani.'

'You're a natural, Ollie,' Imani said to him. 'Anyone can see it.'

Keya, standing beside her, gave a gleeful nod.

'If I may,' said Aunt Fay, 'Ollie seems a trifle reluctant.'

Ollie almost melted with relief, grateful to Aunt Fay for coming to his rescue.

But then she finished the point she'd started making. 'As far as I'm concerned that makes him the ideal candidate,' she said.

'In my experience, anyone who *desires* leadership should automatically be disqualified from the job.'

Jack looked at Ollie triumphantly. 'Well?' she asked him. 'What do you say?'

Ollie stared back at her helplessly, never feeling less like a leader. He looked at Sol and Keya and all the others, then cast his gaze to the vaulted ceiling above their heads. He smiled then, in spite of everything, and opened his mouth to give his answer.

READ ON –
OLLIE'S ADVENTURES
CONTINUE IN ...

✚ PROLOGUE

Errol was already deep into the woods when he heard the monster.

He'd heard rumours of its existence before, of course. Everyone had. It was almost the first thing you learned about when you came to Forest Mount. Most kids pretended not to believe in it (*A monster in the woods? That's kids' stuff, made up by the teachers to scare us into doing what they say*) but Errol knew that everyone did really. He could tell from the way even the older kids peeked out through the dorm windows at night, and jumped at every creaking floorboard and hooting owl.

And now there couldn't be any doubt. Out here, in the dark, all alone, Errol could *feel* that the monster was real. And those were footsteps he'd heard, he was certain. Not human ones, though. Rather, the soft, creeping steps of something that had made the woods its home.

He hurried on, the bobbing torch light at his feet betraying his panic. A tree limb grabbed his backpack and tried to wrench it from him, and after a brief tussle Errol gave it up. There was nothing of any value in the bag anyway. A change of clothes, some rolls stolen from breakfast: nothing worth slowing down for. Everything he treasured – the one thing he treasured, actually: a photograph of his long-lost sister – was in the front pocket of his jeans. If anyone tried to take *that* from him – a demon tree, the monster in the woods, even Colton Crowe, the head pupil and school bully – Errol would have fought back with all the energy he had.

For a moment the thought of his sister gave him courage, and Errol pressed on through the undergrowth with renewed resolve. He would escape. He *would*. And he would find his sister at the place she called the Haven. For days Errol had been planning this, and there was no way he was going to allow himself to fail. Not when he was so close.

In fact he could see it. Could he? The edge of the woods. The shadow of the wall: the final boundary between him and freedom. It was barely twenty, thirty metres ahead.

There was a growl.

Errol stumbled in his fear, almost falling. And then he heard it again. A mean, deep-throated rumble.

He spun, and immediately collided with a tree – one he would have sworn hadn't been there before. The torch he was clutching slipped from his grip. It hit something hard on the forest floor and immediately the beam went out. The only light now came from the moon high above the canopy, which shone down on Errol like a sentry's spotlight.

He started to run . . .

SIMON LELIC IS A WRITER OF CRIME AND THRILLER
NOVELS FOR ADULTS – WINNER OF THE BETTY TRASK AWARD,
SHORTLISTED FOR THE CWA DAGGER AWARDS AND
THE GALAXY NATIONAL BOOK AWARDS.

GHTON WITH HIS WIFE AND
ER THAN HIS FAMILY, READING IS
HE ALSO HOLDS A BLACK BELT
HICH HE TRAINS DAILY.

MON_LELIC